Samuel French Acting Edition

The Open Hand

by Robert Caisley

FOR PRODUCTION ENQUIRIES

UNITED STATES AND CANADA

Info@SamuelFrench.com

1-866-598-8449

UNITED KINGDOM AND EUROPE

Plays@SamuelFrench.co.uk

020-7255-4302

Each title is subject to availability from Samuel French, depending upon country of performance. Please be aware that *THE OPEN HAND* may not be licensed by Samuel French in your territory. Professional and amateur producers should contact the nearest Samuel French office or licensing partner to verify availability.

publisher. No one shall upload this title(s), or part of this title(s), to any social media websites.

For all enquiries regarding motion picture, television, and other media rights, please contact Samuel French.

MUSIC USE NOTE

Licensees are solely responsible for obtaining formal written permission from copyright owners to use copyrighted music in the performance of this play and are strongly cautioned to do so. If no such permission is obtained by the licensee, then the licensee must use only original music that the licensee owns and controls. Licensees are solely responsible and liable for all music clearances and shall indemnify the copyright owners of the play(s) and their licensing agent, Samuel French, against any costs, expenses, losses and liabilities arising from the use of music by licensees. Please contact the appropriate music licensing authority in your territory for the rights to any incidental music.

IMPORTANT BILLING AND CREDIT REQUIREMENTS

If you have obtained performance rights to this title, please refer to your licensing agreement for important billing and credit requirements.

THE OPEN HAND was commissioned by the Clarence Brown Theatre (Calvin MacLean, Producing Artistic Director; David Bryant Byrd, Managing Director) in Knoxville, Tennessee. The world premiere opened on March 30, 2016. The director was Calvin MacLean, with scenic and projection design by Nevena Prodanovic, lighting design by Tannis Kapell, costume design by Marianne Custer, and sound design by Rick Peeples. The stage manager was Alex Ross. The cast was as follows:

ALLISON . . . . Lindsay Nance

JACK . . . . Steve Sherman

FREYA . . . . Melissa David

TODD . . . . Kyle Maxwell

DAVID NATHAN BRIGHT . . . . Rick Peeples

CHARACTERS

ALLISON

JACK – her fiancé

FREYA – her friend

TODD – Freya's husband

All are in their late-twenties/early-thirties.

DAVID NATHAN BRIGHT – an elegant man in his fifties

SETTING

The city.

The present.

Everything is very simply suggested.

Scene changes should take place in full view of the audience.

The intermission falls after Scene Six.

ACKNOWLEDGEMENTS

The Open Hand was written following a series of workshops held at the Clarence Brown Theatre with the director and students in the MFA program at the University of Tennessee-Knoxville. The workshop members were: Calvin MacLean, Brian Gligor, Drew Drake, Cynthia Anne Roser, Erik Johnson, Kyle Maxwell, Melissa David, Lindsay Nance, and Steve Sherman. Clarence Brown Theatre's new play program is made possible by the generous support of Townes Lavidge Osborn and Jenny Banner.

The author wishes to thank the following people for their assistance during the subsequent development of this play: Calvin MacLean, Jere Hodgin, Nan Barnett, Jordana Fraider and the National New Play Network, Christy Montour-Larson, Larry Loebell, Jeni Mahoney and the Seven Devils Playwrights Conference, Allison Siko, Dwayne Blackaller, Steven J. Burge, Simon Brooking, SuzAnne Barabas, Gabor Barabas, Joel Stone and New Jersey Repertory Company, Bryan Fonseca, and Phoenix Theatre. A very special thank you to the Idaho Commission on the Arts and the National Endowment for the Arts for their generous support during the writing of this play.

For Cal

ACT ONE

Scene One

(*An upscale Nepalese restaurant.* **ALLISON** *and* **FREYA** *have just finished lunch. The check is on the table, and only some unused silverware and their water glasses remain. They are old friends and we sense this right away. There is a gift-wrapped present placed precisely between them, with a balloon tied to it. It partially obscures their vision of one another, so that when* **FREYA** *finally speaks, she has to crane her head to one side in order to have line-of-sight with her friend.*)

FREYA. What is that?

ALLISON. Open it.

FREYA. I thought we agreed. No presents!

ALLISON. It's not a present.

     (**FREYA** *regards the package.*)

FREYA. It has a bow on it.

     (**ALLISON** *reaches over and pulls the bow off.*)

It's gift-wrapped. In festive paper. There's a *balloon.*

     (**ALLISON** *takes up her fork and pops the balloon.*)

ALLISON. Shut up and open it.

FREYA. My birthday's a month away. Shouldn't I be giving *you* a present?

ALLISON. (*Cutting her off.*) Freya!

It's not a present.

(**FREYA** *tears off the wrapping. It's a very nice leather planner.*)

ALLISON. *(Cont.)* A good luck charm. For your interview.

(**FREYA** *looks at her disapprovingly.*)

They were having a sale, okay?

FREYA. This violates the pact –

ALLISON. – The pact is still in effect.

FREYA. You changed the terms – how's that fair?

ALLISON. This interview's a big deal for you, so *this* is…an attempt to influence the universe, you know *karm*-ically. Which is *different* than a stupid birthday I get every year.

FREYA. You and birthdays. Bizarre!

ALLISON. Jack swore an oath he wouldn't *do* anything. So you can't either. Swear!

FREYA. How did his big meeting go?

ALLISON. Don't change the subject – swear!
It was all Jack could do to convince me about this little "get-together" Friday. But he's got the tasting next week, so…
I pimped us out as his guinea pigs.

FREYA. Is he doing those little puff pastry things?

ALLISON. Uh-huh.

FREYA. Pimp away!

(*Quick beat.*)

ALLISON. So um…is Todd going to make it?

FREYA. Who?

ALLISON. Your husband –

FREYA. Oh that guy!

ALLISON. I can't remember the last time I saw him.

FREYA. *(Unconvinced.)* I watched him put it in his phone, so –

ALLISON. He can't be *that* busy. Don't car salesmen stand around most of the time *spitballing?*

FREYA. That was Ford, this is Lexus.

ALLISON. I liked Ford Todd better.

> *(There is a pause.* FREYA *sips her water.)*

How are you guys?

> *(But* FREYA *is looking at the smart gift* ALLISON *bought her.)*

FREYA. Seriously, why did you do this? You didn't have to do this. Thanks – you shouldn't have done this.

ALLISON. Thank me by getting the job.
It's this afternoon, right?

FREYA. Yeah, in about… *(She checks the clock on her phone.)* Oh, shit, I should go. Let me get the check.

ALLISON. *(Grabbing the check.)* Don't worry about it, just go.

FREYA. Aaagh! Is it raining now? I just had my hair done.

ALLISON. Go!

FREYA. *(Re: check.)* Ya sure?

ALLISON. You get the next one.

FREYA. Lunch *and* a present?

ALLISON. It's not a present. And don't forget Friday.

FREYA. Your pact, by the way? Your pact is bullshit.

ALLISON. Swear!
I mean it, I'll be really pissed –

FREYA. All right, all right –

ALLISON. And Jack would be super-embarrassed.

FREYA. *(Raises her hand; an oath.)* No presents! I swear.

> *(They kiss.)*

> *(*FREYA *leaves.)*

> *(*ALLISON *glances at the check and then rummages in her bag for her wallet. She can't find it. She rummages some more. She checks her pockets. Nothing.)*

ALLISON. Shit!

> *(She takes out her phone and places a call. We can hear it ringing on the other end through the phone.)*

ALLISON. *(Cont.)* Pick up, pick up.

    (The call goes to voicemail.)

Damn it!

    (She tries texting the same number, then sips her water and glances around the restaurant.)

    (A man appears.)

D.N.B. Hello.

    *(**DAVID NATHAN BRIGHT** is in his fifties, well-groomed, impeccably dressed; has an air of distinction. He wears a top coat and carries an umbrella.)*

ALLISON. Hi…

D.N.B. I can see you're in an uncomfortable position. I'd like to help.

    (He takes out his wallet.)

ALLISON. Oh, no –

    (He places cash on the table.)

I can't allow you to do that.

D.N.B. It's nothing.

ALLISON. I think my fiancé's just in a meeting or something – he usually picks up right away, so…

    (Beat.)

D.N.B. It's really my pleasure. Please allow me.

ALLISON. Do I know you?

D.N.B. It's good isn't it?

ALLISON. Sorry?

D.N.B. *(Re: her plate.)* The dumplings? You had the *Sha Momo.*

ALLISON. Err – yeah.

D.N.B. It's my favorite. I get it every time.

ALLISON. Look, can I –?

D.N.B. It's starting to rain again. Can I flag down a cab for you?

ALLISON. Thank you, no –

D.N.B. Then take this.

> *(He hands her his umbrella. Even though she's shaking her head, she involuntarily accepts it.)*

Have a nice day.

> *(**ALLISON** starts to object, but he is already gone. She looks at the umbrella in her hand, the cash on the table. A beat.)*
>
> *(Now her cell phone starts to ring.)*
>
> *(She sits there holding the phone as it rings.)*
>
> *(The scene shifts.)*

Scene Two

*(We are now in **JACK** and **ALLISON**'s apartment. She's on the couch; he enters with a juicer pitcher filled with some sliced fruit. There is an overnight suitcase by the door. Mid-conversation:)*

JACK. Okay: what do you call those things in Hawaii?

ALLISON. Volcanoes?

JACK. No, the – the things, the –

ALLISON. Hula skirts?

JACK. No, come on be serious – that you *sit* on? *Outside* – you know, off people's living rooms, like a deck…

ALLISON. Lanais?

JACK. *Right*, one of those – he had one of those – it was *so* cool – with this amazing view of the park, and I'm like: *nervous as shit* because this is – this *guy* – you know, this guy has the ability to write me a blank check right there, and all he's been talking about through*out* lunch, the *whole* time, is "What's your favorite movie, what are your favorite books? Is there an artist you like to collect?"

ALLISON. Collect?

JACK. Right? – and so, what do you say? "Yeah, the one from Bed Bath & Beyond."

ALLISON. He's interested in you –

JACK. No, I get it –

ALLISON. – in getting to know you *aside* from your business plan, your menus, your –

JACK. No, I know, 'cause get this: he suddenly shifts gears so *imperceptibly* that I'm like, still yammering on about some Iñárritu flick I've actually never seen or whatever, and he's off on this new tangent: How he wants to maybe *invest* in me. You know, in the restaurant.

ALLISON. That's fantastic.

JACK. Right? Right, so, yeah. *(He exits briefly and we hear the juicer whirring offstage. He has to raise his voice above the* *noise.)* And listen honey, I'm sorry I didn't pick up right away, but –

ALLISON. What?

JACK. *(Offstage.)* When you called –?

ALLISON. It's fine.

JACK. *(Offstage.)* I didn't want to – you know…

ALLISON. I get it – forget it.

JACK. *(Offstage.)* …my phone going off and shit. At like *the* worst possible time imaginable.

ALLISON. It all worked out.

> *(JACK re-enters, with greenish juice in the pitcher. He maybe takes his first breath of the scene right here.)*
>
> *(He smiles.)*

JACK. I was pretty awesome, Al.

ALLISON. Say more.

JACK. I was pretty fucking spectacularly awesome! I think I *nailed* it. I mean I really did. *(He takes a sip from the pitcher.)* And…and every follow-up question the guy had, I was like: *boom!*

ALLISON. I'm proud of you.

JACK. *(Re: the juice.)* You want some of this?

> *(She grimaces and shakes her head "no.")*

It was great, but you know, I'm sure this guy meets a dozen guys like me a week, so.

ALLISON. But your concept – no, don't do that to yourself.

JACK. I know, I'm just saying – I don't wanna get all…

ALLISON. *And* the food to back it up.

> *(He pours himself a glass of juice.)*

JACK. Well, that was my Monday.

What about you? How was lunch? Freya okay?

ALLISON. So what's the next step? Do you know, or what?

JACK. Huh?

ALLISON. With the *guy* – yeah, she's good.

JACK. Well, we discussed…

ALLISON. Todd's selling Lexus now, apparently. Oh, the Nepalese place: great recommendation. Thank Zenna for me.

JACK. Yeah, I know.

ALLISON. You've been there?

JACK. No, about Todd.

ALLISON. You saw Todd? The elusive Todd?

JACK. Saw him a couple weeks back. With one of his customers, I guess. Forget where. Downtown. *Some*where. *(Beat.)* Yeah, so, he's going to look at the numbers or whatever…

ALLISON. Todd?

JACK. No, the guy. And um – I don't know, I guess we could know something by week's end.

ALLISON. That quick?

JACK. The guy's like – *(He snaps his fingers a couple times.)* – no-fucking-nonsense. Actually I think he's ADHD. He was on his phone and tablet the whole time. At one point I think he said something in Mandarin Chinese.

ALLISON. You wheeler-dealer, you!
Come here.

(He does. He sits, drinks his juice.)

JACK. I'm spinning.

ALLISON. I'm so proud of you, Jack.

JACK. It hasn't happened yet.

ALLISON. It's going to.

(She kisses him.)

Thanks for the postcard.

JACK. Sorry I didn't mail it from there.
Or write anything on it.

ALLISON. You were busy.

JACK. Don't move.

(*JACK quickly goes to his suitcase and takes a pen.
He writes on her postcard and hands it to her.*)

ALLISON. (*She reads it, and smiles.*) Did you? Wish I was there?

(*He draws close to her.*)

JACK. "I do not love you except because I love you."

(*This is a thing with them.*)

ALLISON. "I do not love you except because I love you" too.

(*They kiss. Not a short one.*)

(*Then.*)

JACK. (*Out of left field.*) Todd hates it at Lexus.

ALLISON. What?

JACK. He only took it because the money was – *you know* – and Freya is lookin' at that *house* – but I guess the pressure is nuts, and he's got this *fucking boss* always on his ass.

Aaagh, I shouldn't have said that!

Don't tell Freya!

ALLISON. Hey, hey – what are you doing? You had a good trip. You had a good day. Stay in a good spot.

JACK. I don't know why I thought about that.

ALLISON. They're not us.

This is us.

(*Beat.*)

Come on. Open some wine.

JACK. The good stuff?

ALLISON. (*Playful reprimand.*) No! Save that for Friday.

JACK. (*Playing dumb.*) What's Friday?

ALLISON. Good boy!

JACK. I don't deserve you.

ALLISON. Say that again?

JACK. I don't deserve you.

ALLISON. Just one more time?

> (*JACK playfully attacks* **ALLISON** *on the couch,
> and gets poked in the back by an umbrella.*)

JACK. I. Don't. Deser – Ow!

> (*JACK holds up the umbrella. It's the one* **DAVID
> NATHAN BRIGHT** *gave to* **ALLISON** *in Scene
> One.*)

ALLISON. (*Snatching it from him.*) That's Freya's.
She left it at lunch.

> (*He shows us a little bit of his behind.*)

JACK. Do I have a bruise?

> (**ALLISON** *takes the umbrella and places it in a tall
> vase by the door.*)

ALLISON. If you're lucky, I'll kiss it better later.

> (*He pauses briefly, then.*)

JACK. Is it later yet?

ALLISON. (*One of those kinda laughs.*) Ha-ha.

JACK. Hey – you never told me: what happened with the
check?

ALLISON. What check?

JACK. For lunch? How'd you end up paying? They make
you wash dishes or something?

ALLISON. I had some cash. As it turned out…
Tucked away in my bag. Thank god. So –

JACK. Good. I hate letting you down.

ALLISON. You didn't let me down.

> (*Brief pause.*)

Hey.
Guess what time it is?
It's later.

> (*The scene shifts.*)

Scene Three

(FREYA and TODD's place. They are sort of having breakfast. FREYA works a French press; there's a plate of fruit on the counter. TODD is walking in and out of the room as he gets dressed. On the table is the leather planner that ALLISON gave to FREYA in Scene One.)

FREYA. You think she forgot?

TODD. *(From offstage.)* What?

FREYA. That I gave it to her?
Well, not to her, *per se*, but you know. To him.

(TODD enters.)

TODD. *(Re: tie choices.)* Blue? Or red?

FREYA. Wasn't that long ago.
A year maybe?
Drink your coffee.
It's *weird.*

(TODD inspects the leather planner.)

TODD. Maybe it's not the same one.

FREYA. It is the same one.

TODD. Maybe this is a different one.

(She takes it from him.)

FREYA. No, I remember because when I picked it out for Jack I wondered if I should get a second one for you.

TODD. So we'd be matching?
Gee, how cute.

(He eats a slice of pear.)

(His cell phone chirps. A text.)

TODD. Maybe this is the same *kind* of one but not the *actual* same one.

FREYA. It's the same.

TODD. Okay, Sherlock.

FREYA. It is.

TODD. *(Pear munching.)* So?

FREYA. So: nothing.

TODD. Something.

FREYA. I'm trying to work out if Allison *knew* she was re-gifting…or if she just *spaced it* – you know – and went to that shelf in the closet we all have.

TODD. *(More pear munching.)* There's a closet?

FREYA. Yes. Where we keep the crap we get that we don't want and then try to pass it off next time we have a gifting obligation.

TODD. Yeah, I don't know if everyone's brain works that way.

FREYA. Yes they do.

TODD. When I get crap I don't want I throw it out.

FREYA. That's wasteful.

TODD. And has the added advantage of getting rid of crap I don't want. Eat some pear.

FREYA. Have you ever thrown out anything I gave you?

TODD. What was the question?

FREYA. Todd?!

TODD. There are some things a man must take to the grave.

FREYA. Drink your coffee.

> *(But he's busy changing his tie again.)*

How could she forget a thing like that?
She's normally quite detail-oriented.
I wonder if Jack knows she re-gifted *his gift?*
She has been distracted lately.
With her birthday.

TODD. You're not supposed to say that.

FREYA. It's perverse.

She makes such a big deal about her birthday *not being* her birthday, because it has the exact *opposite* effect and

everyone makes an even *bigger* deal about her birthday.
It's classic Allison.

TODD. *(Re-enters.)* Excuse me?

FREYA. By mitigating the generosity of others, she gets to
sidestep it herself.

TODD. *(To **ALLISON**'s defense.)* That's not why she does it.

FREYA. Why does she do it?

> (**TODD** *just looks at her.*)

TODD. *(A different tie.)* What about this one?

FREYA. Wear the one I got you for Christmas.

TODD. You got me one for Christmas?

> (**FREYA** *glares at him as he exits once again.*)

FREYA. Shut up. Drink your coffee.

TODD. *(From offstage.)* It's *cold.*

> (**FREYA** *warms up his coffee.* **TODD** *gets another
> text.*)

FREYA. *(Re: **TODD**'s phone.)* Jesus, it's not even seven-thirty.

TODD. *(Crossing through the room.)* Where are my car keys?

FREYA. On the thing.

> (*He goes to find his car keys on the thing.*)

TODD. *(Offstage.)* Did they call you yet? The *French?*

FREYA. *(Distracted.)* No.

TODD. *(Offstage.)* When will they call you?

FREYA. Huh?

TODD. *(Offstage.)* About the job?

FREYA. They had one more candidate.
  (But this is still gnawing at her.) Here's what I think…

TODD. *(Offstage.)* Where did you –? Never mind.

> (*He returns with car keys in hand.*)

FREYA. …We arranged to have lunch.
  She knew I was going on this interview.
  She wanted to give me a gift. But she didn't have time.
  So she went to her closet.

And she grabbed *this*, which is appropriate, right?

And she wrapped it up. *Knowing* that her *own* birthday was looming – her *non*-birthday.

But she'd also put out this *fiat*…that "None Shall Buy Me Presents." And this was the wrench in the works that messed up the whole dynamic and put *me* in a really fucking awkward situation. I would not know what to do this Friday and so would show up – gift in hand – for fear of appearing heartless, *regardless* of the No Gift Mandate, but *Allison* would still be all "Oh no you shouldn't have." Well, guess what? I'm not taking a gift. That'll teach her!

> *(***TODD*** *was about to eat a slice of pear, but he's just standing there with his mouth open, staring at her.)*

TODD. Wow. I don't know where your brain finds the energy to do what you just did.

FREYA. The scales, Todd! The scales have to be even! *(He just looks at her.)* What?

> *(***TODD*** *shakes his head "nothing" and crosses out of the room again. He returns with yet another tie choice.)*

I'm just saying, if you're going to re-gift you've got to keep notes or something. Right? Like a *chart*.

So you don't forget shit.

TODD. You forget shit.

FREYA. No I don't.

TODD. You forget shit all the time.

FREYA. Like what?

TODD. *(On second thought.)* Okay. You don't.

FREYA. No, Todd, like what?

What shit do I forget? All the time.

TODD. *(A Zen thing.)* No, I changed my mind, I'm now saying you *don't* forget shit. Like ever. *(Re: tie.)* What about the grey?

FREYA. All your ties are the same, Todd.

TODD. No they're not.

FREYA. They're all various shades of blue, red or grey – all various *patterns*, in blue, grey, red. Your closet is an endless variety of exactly *the same fucking thing*.

TODD. *(Eggshells.)* Okay, then: blue.

FREYA. *(Suddenly vicious.)* – And what is the big deal today? What's with the *ties?*

Stop fucking around with the ties, pick one already!

TODD. I have a meeting.

FREYA. A meeting? A *car* meeting?

What do you talk about anyway?

Cars?

TODD. Yeah.

FREYA. *(Caveman voice.)* "Sold bunch of cars last month. This month, must sell more."

> *(He laughs.)*

Don't laugh – I'm angry.

> *(He yanks off the tie he was wearing and starts to exit.)*

Don't walk away!

> *(He instantly returns, stands very close to her.)*

What??

TODD. I don't like cilantro!

I don't like cilantro. Okay?

It tastes like soap.

I told you this on our second date or something – but you forgot.

FREYA. No I didn't –

TODD. – Yeah. You always forget.

You put it in everything –

FREYA. No I don't.

TODD. – In *almost* everything. Even shit you shouldn't put cilantro in, you put it in. And you act surprised when I say, "Is there cilantro in this?" You make this…*face.*

FREYA. What face?

TODD. *That* face. The naïve cilantro face.

FREYA. Why are we talking about cilantro?

TODD. It's a little thing. But it's a big thing.

FREYA. Cilantro is a big thing?

TODD. It is to me.

(*Trying to calm down.*) …Never mind.

(*Exits briefly.*)

FREYA. (*Like a little kid.*) I like cilantro.

TODD. (*Dashing back on.*) That's the point I was trying to make.

…But I'll shut up now, because that's what Zoe wants us to work on, right? Figuring out how we go from *zero* to Go Fuck Yourself in like ten seconds flat. So I'm looking for ways to scale back my feelings.

FREYA. Do you not want to go anymore?

TODD. Look –

FREYA. To Zoe?

TODD. That's not what I – Zoe's fine – but you've gotta…

Baby, you've gotta start putting some of her exercises into action. Because you spin shit right into outer space.

FREYA. …

TODD. Do you like the leather planner?

(**FREYA** *nods.*)

Do you think it was a nice gesture?

(**FREYA** *nods again.*)

Do you want to make Allison feel badly that it may or may not have been the very same planner you gave Jack last year for his…whatever the hell it was?

FREYA. His review in *Food & Wine.* And no.

TODD. Would it make you feel better if they'd said to you a year ago: "Oh thanks – but yeah – we don't *like* or *need* this so we'll probably be re-gifting it at some point in the future?"

FREYA. No. I don't know. I guess, no.

TODD. Okay – so is it the *thing* itself or the *gesture?*
Which? *Which?*
She also bought your lunch on Monday – if I recall –
and now you're quibbling over the gift she may or may
not have recycled –

FREYA. *(With certainty.)* – It's recycled.

TODD. *(He exhales. It's a Zen thing.)* Freya. I love you.
I'm not ending the conversation.
I'm just ending the argument.

> (**FREYA** *looks at him. He's right.*)

FREYA. The grey is nice with that suit.

> *(He switches to the grey tie.)*

TODD. I have to go… I have a meeting. I do not want to
attend this meeting. For I know what is to *transpire*:
the newly *anointed* sales manager will unveil the master
plan for how to drive up competition.

FREYA. How?

TODD. Putting another guy on the floor.

FREYA. Aren't there four of you already? Already exceeding
your quotas?

TODD. Well, now there's five fighting over the same car-
cass.

> (**TODD***'s phone goes off again.)*

FREYA. Who keeps texting you?

TODD. The Universe. Telling me I'm on the wrong track.

FREYA. Ha-ha.

TODD. It's Jack.

FREYA. Oh shit – I forgot – he's reminding you about Friday
night. I was supposed to say something. Can you go?

TODD. Friday –?

FREYA. – Can you? To Allison's bir… – her "get-together"?

TODD. I'll try.

FREYA. Try hard.

> *(They look at each other. A moment.)*

TODD. Have some pear. It's good for you.

> *(He kisses her on the forehead, and exits.)*
>
> *(The scene changes.)*

Scene Four

(The light is different. **DAVID NATHAN BRIGHT** *is sitting on a park bench with his morning coffee and paper.* **ALLISON** *jogs on. She's wearing workout clothes and has earbuds in. We can faintly hear the music playing. She sees him.)*

ALLISON. Hello.

D.N.B. Morning.

(He keeps reading his paper. She takes her earbuds out and turns off her phone.)

ALLISON. You don't remember me. Do you?

D.N.B. Sorry. Have we met?

ALLISON. From the restaurant?

D.N.B. Err –

ALLISON. The Nepalese?

(He still doesn't know.)

I was the dumpling.
Who couldn't pay for her food.

(He laughs.)

D.N.B. Yes. I'm sorry. Of course.
How are you?

ALLISON. Great. And you?

D.N.B. You look quite different.

*(***ALLISON*** regards herself.)*

How was your run?

ALLISON. More of a controlled fall.

(He laughs.)

D.N.B. Well, it was very nice seeing you again.

ALLISON. You too.

(He goes back to reading his paper. She does a knee-bend or something.)

ALLISON. *(Cont.)* I've never seen you in the park before.

D.N.B. I've never seen you either.

ALLISON. I live nearby. Do you live nearby?

D.N.B. Not really.

ALLISON. *(Glancing around the park.)* It's nice here. We've got a bit of a homeless problem. At night. But yeah…

> *(He smiles. Nods. Goes back to reading his paper.)*

Well, I won't keep you.

> *(She looks like she's about to jog off, but…)*

Actually. I never got the chance to –
(Re: the bench.) Do you mind?

D.N.B. Please.

> *(He takes a handkerchief from his pocket and cleans off the park bench for her to sit.)*

ALLISON. I'm sorry, is this rude? You're reading your paper, and I –

D.N.B. It's all bad news, anyway.

ALLISON. – I'm Allison, by the way.

D.N.B. Nice to meet you, Allison.

> *(She thinks he might volunteer his own name, but he doesn't.)*

ALLISON. What you did at the restaurant?

D.N.B. It's nothing.

ALLISON. No. It was very kind, and…well, I don't have any money on me right now –

D.N.B. – I'm not expecting you to pay me back.

ALLISON. – I insist –

D.N.B. It's not necessary. I told you. It was my pleasure.

ALLISON. But I want to set things right.
When I told my boyf – my fiancé…he was mortified that some *stranger* had to rescue me. So, I would like to –

D.N.B. There's nothing to set right.

> *(Quick pause.)*

ALLISON. I never got a chance to thank you – properly, I mean – I sat there like an idiot, and you left before I could…

I don't even know your name.

D.N.B. Allison, you really don't have to. It was nothing. It was my absolute pleasure.

ALLISON. What *is* your name?

D.N.B. David Nathan Bright.

ALLISON. David.

You don't know me.

You don't know anything about me.

D.N.B. I don't need to know someone to offer them a little assistance. Which is what it was: a *little* assistance.

ALLISON. It was an $80 check.

D.N.B. The dumplings *were* really good, though, weren't they?

> *(They share a laugh.)*

One could make the argument that knowing you might have precluded my wanting to help.

ALLISON. What?

D.N.B. That was a joke.

ALLISON. *(Through laughter.)* Right…well I just wanted to say *thank you.* You did a very nice thing that not many people would have done. I don't think.

D.N.B. Maybe someday you'll get a chance to do it for someone else.

> *(He looks at her. Pause.)*

ALLISON. I should get going. *(She stands, turns, then turns back.)*

Is there…?

> *(He looks up at her.)*

Anything that I could do to…*repay*…the favor?

D.N.B. Yes.

ALLISON. – Tell me.

D.N.B. Enjoy the rest of your day.

And don't give it another thought.

ALLISON. Well, thank you. Again.

> (**ALLISON** *gives a little wave and starts to jog off, but she doesn't get very far before she wheels around and comes back.*)

My mother – okay this is going to sound weird – etiquette was this big deal when we were kids. She insisted that we express our gratitude whenever we received a gift. No matter how small. My brother, he – my *twin* brother and I – were always sending Thank You cards, and it was a total pain in the ass when you're like *ten*…but it's something that stayed with me. Okay, this is also weird – can I have your address?

> (*He laughs. He reaches into his jacket and takes out an elegant business card holder during the following:*)

So I can assuage my childhood guilt, or whatever.

D.N.B. You don't have to do this.

ALLISON. I would like to.

It would make me feel…better.

D.N.B. All right then.

> (*He takes out a pen and writes his information on the back of the card.*)

ALLISON. – *Plus* I won't have my mother's voice reverberating in my head all night. So, you'd be doing me a *double* favor.

Maybe I'll send two cards, kill two birds with one stone.

> (**ALLISON** *laughs at her own weak attempt at humor.*)

> (**DAVID NATHAN BRIGHT** *hands her the card.*)

(*Reads.*) "David Nathan Bright."

D.N.B. You're a twin?

> (**ALLISON** *looks at him. She nods.*)

My details are on the back.

ALLISON. Thank you. Again…and again.

> *(She does a little theatrical bow as she backs away. She turns to walk off, and then suddenly turns back.)*

It's my birthday – not really – on Friday.

And my boyfriend…my fiancé *now* I guess – he wasn't supposed to throw me a party – long story – but one has just sort of spontaneously *occurred*.

It's an unofficial birthday…

A get-together –

Couple of friends –

And if you don't have anything planned…

Would you be our guest?

Jack is, uh, my fiancé, knows his way around a kitchen, so…the food I can guarantee will be top-notch. *(Laughs in advance of her own joke.)* I can't vouch for the conversation.

D.N.B. I do have something. Already. But thank you.

ALLISON. Oh, okay, sure. I figured. Just wanted –

D.N.B. No, it's very kind. Normally I would say yes, but this is special –

ALLISON. – Yeah, sure, no worries –

D.N.B. – friend from Paris in town on business.

ALLISON. *C'est la vie.*

D.N.B. Thank you, though.

ALLISON. Well. Goodbye.

D.N.B. Goodbye.

> *(**ALLISON** puts her earbuds in and starts to jog off, but turns back once more and runs back on.)*

ALLISON. I still have your umbrella.

D.N.B. *(With a smile.)* Keep it.

> *(Lights shift.)*

Scene Five

(Night. Bedroom. A pale-colored light from outside the window illuminates the room. **JACK** *and* **ALLISON** *are moving around under the covers; the start of something intimate. The opening moment should be long enough that the audience becomes slightly uncomfortable. Then let it play a little longer. That's when the scene should begin.)*

ALLISON. *(Popping up out of the blankets.)* Did you call Todd?

JACK. What? No. I will.

ALLISON. He needs to be here Friday.
He's the buffer.

JACK. Okay, can it wait until we're done here?

ALLISON. I don't mean *now*, Jack, I mean soon, like, like tomorrow.

JACK. Right. "Call Todd." Check.

ALLISON. I'm not kidding!

JACK. I'll call him. First thing.

(He gently pulls her back down. Couple seconds, then:)

ALLISON. Because he has to come.

JACK. *(Sighs.)* Yes, I know, can *we?*

ALLISON. I'm worried about those guys. Promise me you'll call?

JACK. What are you doing?
You told *me* not to obsess.

ALLISON. Yes, but now *I'm* obsessing. You shouldn't have told me that Todd hates his job.

JACK. I didn't tell you that Todd hates his job.

ALLISON. What did you tell me?

JACK. That Todd hates his job.

*(***JACK***'s not entirely certain what he needs to say right now, but he knows enough to know he needs to change the subject.)*

(**ALLISON** *climbs out of bed.*)

Look, Al, he mentioned it in passing. It was an off-hand thing – like guys do. What is this about?

ALLISON. (*Snaps.*) This isn't about any birthday. Jesus!
Friday is a "get-together with friends."
Quit mentioning my birthday.

(*She exits. Offstage, a bathroom light snaps on.*)

JACK. Okay!
I didn't.

(**JACK** *drains what's left in his wine glass on the bedside table.*)

Whatever he told me, he told me in confidence. So don't go *blabbing* to Freya, because I only got like a piece of the story.

ALLISON. (*Offstage.*) I'm not gonna blab.

(*Quick pause.*)

JACK. What I've learned –?

ALLISON. (*Offstage.*) I wasn't going to *blab.*

JACK. If it could hurt just as well as help…do nothing!

(**ALLISON** *returns wearing one of* **JACK**'s *shirts.*)

ALLISON. You're right.

JACK. What?

(*She sits on the floor and does something "meditative." A yoga pose?*)

ALLISON. I said you're right.

JACK. Oh. Well. I. Didn't mean to…be.

(*Beat.*)

It's two-thirty. Come back to bed.

ALLISON. (*Softly, because she doesn't mean it.*) No. Fuck off.

JACK. Al. Allison.

ALLISON. I'm meditating.
Stop saying things.

(*He crosses the room; nuzzles in behind her.*)

ALLISON. *(Cont.)* Stop doing things.

JACK. *(Whispers.)* "I do not love you except because I love you."

> *(He kisses her neck. She likes it. She pretends not to like it. The "like it" part wins. She turns toward him as far as her pose will allow and they kiss. It lasts long enough that we think the scene might end here, except this happens:)*

ALLISON. I lied to you.

JACK. What are you talking about?

ALLISON. *(Crossing away.)* Remember when I called you? From lunch –?

JACK. With Freya –?

ALLISON. *(Self-effacing.)* This is so stupid!

JACK. What?

ALLISON. The check came.
I didn't have my wallet.
I told you that I found cash in my bag.
I didn't have cash in my bag.

JACK. Why didn't Freya pay?

ALLISON. She had to run. She had the interview. I was *stuck* there. And you didn't pick up –
And I lied –

JACK. – Help me out.

ALLISON. I lied to you.
It's stupid.
I – was embarrassed.

JACK. This is what you lied about?

> *(She nods, then climbs back into bed.)*

You're weird.

ALLISON. And the fucking *wait staff* were giving me this: "Oh she's one of them" kind of looks across the restaurant.
And you didn't pick up.

And this guy came up.

JACK. What guy?

ALLISON. This *super*-nice guy. And paid for the whole thing.

JACK. Your lunch?

ALLISON. Everything.

JACK. That was nice.

ALLISON. It was very nice.

JACK. Why did he do that?

ALLISON. Because – I don't know – because he just did.

JACK. Yes but why did he do that?

ALLISON. That's what I'm saying.

I felt stupid, but I was kind of in a bind –

JACK. – because I didn't pick up.

ALLISON. Well, yes – but that's not the point – the point is…and it's *dumb*…when you asked me, about it later… I lied.

(Pause.)

JACK. Okay. *(Pause.)* Why?

ALLISON. I don't know.

(JACK laughs.)

JACK. That's funny.

That's a funny thing to lie about.

Don't you think that's funny?

(JACK exits slowly to the bathroom.)

ALLISON. Are you upset with me?

JACK. *(Offstage.)* Why would I be upset?

ALLISON. I know so, why would I lie?

JACK. *(Offstage.)* Did you really think I'd be upset?

(Offstage, the toilet flushes softly.)

ALLISON. I don't know. The whole thing was kind of bizarre.

(JACK wanders back on.)

JACK. That's funny.

>(*Pause as* **JACK** *ruminates on whether it's funny.*)

Was he weird? The guy?

Was he creepy, or…did he make any kind of…?

ALLISON. No.

JACK. Huh.

>(*He climbs back into bed.*)

ALLISON. But it's been this…stressful few days where I, I've been…holding it in. It's dumb.

JACK. You're wonderfully silly.

It's why I love you.

>(*He goes to kiss her, but…*)

ALLISON. I saw him again.

>(*Beat.*)

JACK. The paying guy?

ALLISON. On my run. He was in the park.

JACK. Our park?

What did he want?

ALLISON. He wanted to read his paper.

I wouldn't let him. I wanted – I wanted to thank him.

He wouldn't let me.

>(*There is a pause.*)

JACK. That's funny

>(*They look at each other for a long beat.*)

That you didn't tell me.

ALLISON. I didn't want you to be mad.

JACK. You didn't do anything.

ALLISON. I *withheld.*

>(*Beat.*)

JACK. (*Surprised by this.*) Okay, this is weird: I suddenly feel like an asshole.

ALLISON. Why?

JACK. I wasn't there for you.

> (**ALLISON** *laughs.*)

Why are you laughing?

ALLISON. "I wasn't there for you."

JACK. Yeah?

ALLISON. I don't know, I just don't think people in relationships actually say things like that. In real life. I mean do they? It's kind of cliché.

JACK. I think it's a cliché because it's *true*. Like a *lot* of the time.

ALLISON. I don't think that's the definition of a cliché but okay.

JACK. *(Sudden condemnation.)* You *know* that's why you didn't tell me.

ALLISON. Haven't you been listening? I don't.

JACK. Because you *know* that's how I'd *feel.*
Guilty.

ALLISON. *You* feel guilty?

JACK. – Like a cliché!

> (**JACK** *sighs. Then laughs. He suddenly realizes how dumb the conversation is.*)

ALLISON. What?

JACK. *(Shaking his head slightly.)* This conversation: dumb.
Come here.

> *(But* **ALLISON** *'s into it now.)*

ALLISON. No. Are you upset?
That he paid for my lunch?
Or that I made up some bullshit story instead?

JACK. – I'm not *upset* –

ALLISON. Okay.

JACK. I'm –

ALLISON. What?

JACK. I'm something else.

ALLISON. Something else?

JACK. It's *some* kind of feeling…

ALLISON. Of irritation?

JACK. Kind of – yeah – no. Um, I don't know what it is, I feel… I feel sort of…*stupid.*

ALLISON. Stupid?

You feel stupid?

JACK. Isn't that how you felt? Or lame, or – I don't know.

ALLISON. You feel lame?

JACK. Stop repeating stuff!

I *feeeeeel!*

Look, Allison, you told me this *thing,* okay, and it was weird, it was weird that you lied to me about something that was no big deal, but the fact that you lied about it kinda-sorta makes it a big deal suddenly, okay? And I'm sorting through that, I'm working that particular set of…things, thoughts, *through.*

ALLISON. But you're not mad at me?

JACK. *(Calmly, emphatically.)* Absolutely not.

For what? For not having your wallet?

(Through this: snowball effect.) For calling me at a time that was really inconvenient for me to pick up, so you were left to fend for yourself in a cruel and pitiless world, and instead of *being there* for you, some other guy, some *super-nice* guy – isn't that how you described him? – sweeps in like, fuck I don't know, *Robin* Hood or some shit, and takes care of business?

Am I mad?

Why would I get mad at you for that? That would be peculiar – except that, *fuck,* I think I *am* mad at you.

ALLISON. I'm mad at you too.

JACK. What did I do –?

ALLISON. – Exactly!

> *(A pause of exasperation as they arrive at the weird impasse.)*

What do we do?

(*They looks around the room for the answer. It's not there.*)

Should we have sex?

(*He thinks about it, really philosophically.*)

JACK. Probably.

ALLISON. Okay, then, let's have sex.

(*They make their clumsy way to the bed. They fall in. They start fooling around again. It looks different than it did before. They're both a little self-conscious and not quite sure if they're as "into it" as they should be. But they keep going, with* ALLISON, *if anything, being more of the aggressor. During this:*)

JACK. I'm still mad at you.

ALLISON. I can tell.

JACK. How?

ALLISON. Your lips are stiffer than usual.
Don't stop.

(*Moaning, kissing.*)

JACK. My lips are *stiffer?*

ALLISON. There's a…*rigidity*, I don't know, it's subtle.

(*More moaning, kissing.*)

JACK. I feel like we're not done talking about this.

ALLISON. (*She gives him a whack on the back.*) Stay focused.

(*They're back into it. And some more moaning, kissing.*)

JACK. What's his name?

ALLISON. What?

JACK. Robin Hood.

ALLISON. I don't remember.

JACK. You don't remember?

Guy paid for your lunch and you don't remember his n–?

ALLISON. I forget! David… Something-Something.

JACK. David Something-Something?

ALLISON. He had three names, okay?

> (*He's about to kiss her, again, but…*)

JACK. Like aliases?

ALLISON. No, like John Wilkes Booth.
Focus.

> (**JACK** *tries to focus. He can't focus.*)

JACK. I feel like – Like he's here…in the *room*. John Wilkes Booth.

ALLISON. All he did was pay for my lunch.

JACK. Why did you lie to me?

ALLISON. I already told you I don't know.

JACK. And that's really *unspecific*…and annoying.

> (**JACK** *exhales, stands up, and roams around the room.*)

What does he do, this guy? How old is he? Is he an old guy, this guy, or what?
Are you telling me *everything*?
Are you telling me everything that transpired –?
At the restaurant –?
In the park –?

ALLISON. Are you accusing me of something?

JACK. I don't know yet – (*Instant retraction.*) – I don't know why I said that.

> (*Brief pause.*)

ALLISON. Yes!
I told you everything!
Happy?

JACK. Did you?

ALLISON. Yes.

(Beat.)

No.

Shit!

JACK. What?

Allison –?

ALLISON. He gave me his card.

(She grabs the business card from the bedside table.)

JACK. Oh my god it's *right* there!

(He reads:)

"David Nathan Bright."

Sounds like an assassin.

ALLISON. I invited him.

To dinner.

Friday.

JACK. Why?

ALLISON. To thank him.

JACK. I know but *why Friday?*

ALLISON. To repay him.

For his generosity.

JACK. It's your *birthday* –

ALLISON. IT'S NOT MY BIRTHDAY!!

(She moves across the room. She now drains the wine in her own glass and refills it. She sits on the edge of the bed, nervously sipping wine.)

JACK. Sorry, I know. I'm sorry.

ALLISON. It's a casual "get together."

With a couple of friends.

So you can test out your new *whatevers.*

I just need to put things right with this guy.

JACK. You're right.

And *I'd* like to thank him too. Actually. In person.

So. Yeah. Plan approved.

That would alleviate my – *whatever* it is I'm feeling.

ALLISON. Except he didn't accept. Had a prior engagement.

JACK. He can't do that.

He has to come.

I've wrapped my head around this thing now, so…

Call him. Can you call him?

ALLISON. It's two-thirty in the morning.

JACK. Tomorrow. First thing. I call Todd. You call –?

ALLISON. David Nathan Bright.

JACK. David Nathan Bright.

ALLISON. He already said no, Jack.

> (**JACK** *has a little man-tantrum.*)

JACK. GAAAAAAAGGGGGHHHHHH!!

ALLISON. What?? What is it?

JACK. I don't want this guy being one up on me. I know it's illogical, but that's how I feel.

ALLISON. I'll call him, okay?

First thing.

Please. Come back to bed.

> (*They climb back into bed.* **JACK** *clicks off the light. Moonlight. They both just lay there. Motionless. Ten seconds.*)

JACK. I can't sleep.

ALLISON. Me neither.

JACK. Call him.

> (*She turns to him.*)

Call him now.

> (*We hear rainfall.*)

> (*The lights begins to shift, and in the transition between the scenes we hear* **ALLISON**'s *voicemail message begin.*)

ALLISON. (*Voice-over.*) Hi.

David.

This is Allison.

From the restaurant.

From the park.

Dumpling Allison. Umbrella Allison.

I know it's late.

About Friday.

If you change your mind, or plans...we're at 2217 Franklin. Apartment 3G.

Seven o'clock.

Oh. And...everything's provided.

> *(The sound of the rain gets louder and louder until it drowns everything else out.)*

Scene Six

> *(Friday night. **JACK** and **ALLISON**'s apartment. The space has been rearranged so it's easy for people to walk around and sample the tapas **JACK** has prepared and is right now serving out on little plates around the dining table. **ALLISON** has a bottle of wine and wine key in her hands. Mid-conversation.)*

ALLISON. I can't believe you!

JACK. – I *kinda* forgot –

ALLISON. – How can you *kinda* forget –?

JACK. – By sort of not remembering.

ALLISON. All you had to do was call him, text him – he's your best friend. Don't you *communicate?*

JACK. I had the follow-up conference call today, with the restaurant guy – I was pre-occupied.

ALLISON. *(Threatening.)* Todd's the buffer – if Todd doesn't show up –

JACK. *(Grabs phone.)* I'll text him right now.

FREYA. *(Offstage.)* Oh, my god!

> *(**FREYA** enters.)*

I love that thing in the bathroom. Is that new?

ALLISON. You like it?

FREYA. I want one.

ALLISON. I'll give you the catalogue.

FREYA. What are you guys talking about?

JACK. *(Texting.)* The um…

ALLISON. Jack wants to know about your job thing.

JACK. Yes, Jack wants to know about your job thing. You excited?

FREYA. I'm nervous – I'm nuts – I'm cautiously optimistic. They called this morning and it was one of those things, you know, where it sounds like you got the job, but they don't exactly come out and say: "You've got the job." So: pins and needles.

(Re: tapas.) What are these?

JACK. Braised squid with artichokes.

FREYA. *(Suspicious.)* Seriously?

ALLISON. You're gonna love it.

> (**FREYA** *tastes the squid. It's delicious.*)

What I tell ya?

JACK. So what is it again? Some cruise line?

> (*But* **FREYA**'s *helped herself to more squid, so* **ALLISON** *answers.*)

ALLISON. *L'Odyssée. (To* **FREYA***)* Did I get that right?

FREYA. *(Re:* **ALLISON**'s *accent.) Tres bien!*

ALLISON. College. All four years.

FREYA. They basically want to challenge Cunard and Viking and, you know, the big guys –

JACK. – Uhuh –

FREYA. – in the world-wide luxury cruise market. And, uh – yeah.

ALLISON. I knew you were going to get it –

FREYA. – I *might* get it –

ALLISON. – No, I'm serious, at lunch, when you were telling me about it, I thought, "This is Freya, to a T!" And all week – you think I'm kidding – I've been picturing you in this big office.

> (*She does a funny thing with her hands like she's picturing* **FREYA** *in a big office.*)

FREYA. They *do* have amazing offices, actually. The woman who interviewed me…so fucking classy… Pauline Chatagnier – isn't that a great name –? I asked her what it meant and she said…"chestnut tree"… "It's someone who lives near a tree, that grows chestnuts." I love the French!

JACK. *(Popping a cork on a bottle.)* So you'd be doing sort of the same thing?

FREYA. Basically.
Except. It's like…selecting all the wines for this *really*
high-end restaurant.
With *every* menu conceivable.
That *floats.*
All over the world.
Like *fifteen* of them.

JACK. Wow.

FREYA. Yeah.

JACK. That's fantastic.

ALLISON. *(To* JACK.*)* Right?

FREYA. It's a huge step up.

JACK. I'll drink to that.

   (They clink glasses.)

FREYA. Which is why I made an offer on the house.

ALLISON. You made an offer?

FREYA. It's a surprise *(To* JACK.*)* so mum's the word… *(Back
to* ALLISON.*) if* he ever shows up. They've been restruc-
turing the sales force at work, and you know Todd, he's
agonizing, endlessly stressed, he's the very best they've
got, so I think this is his moment, his moment to *shine.*

   *(*JACK *peers at* ALLISON *over the rim of his wine
   glass.)*

ALLISON. This is your year. I can feel it.

FREYA. Well, they haven't sent a contract yet. But that's the
French, isn't it? All about the formality: all so *de rigueur.*

ALLISON. Well, I'm celebrating in advance, even if you're
hedging.
And *Jack's* thing…

JACK. OK, OK!

ALLISON. What is it with you two? The most talented people
I know…for some *incomprehensible* reason neither one
of you feels deserving of any good fortune.

JACK. *(Gives her a peck on the cheek.)* Pot, kettle.

FREYA. I don't want to jinx it by talking too much.
(She smiles.) But I'm pretty excited. Like –

*(***FREYA*** *receives a text.)*

– like "I'm going to swallow my own *tongue* excited"
when the official offer comes in. Right now, it's just too
surreal.

ALLISON. *(Re: text message.)* Is that Todd? Is he coming?

FREYA. *(Forced smile.)* He better be, or I'll fucking kill him.

ALLISON. *(Glaring at* JACK.*)* Tell me about it.

FREYA. "Happy face!"
More wine?

*(***FREYA*** *reaches for a bottle, but…)*

JACK. *(Takes the bottle.)* Ah-ah, that's for my toast later.

ALLISON. *(Claps her hands like a kid.)* He's been saving it for
little old me.

FREYA. *(She inspects the label.)* Not bad, little old you.

*(***JACK*** *hands her something he's already opened.)*

JACK. Try this. Pairs better with the chorizo.

FREYA. Chor*izo*! Todd's fave. Serves him right if there's
none left.

ALLISON. Good old Jacko here forgot to call him.

FREYA. What?

ALLISON. I already yelled at him.

JACK. She did. She already yelled at me.

ALLISON. Jack was supposed to remind Todd.

JACK. Kinda forgot, sorry.

FREYA. No, he got your texts the other day.

*(***JACK*** *and* ***ALLISON*** *share a look.)*

At zero-dark-fucking-thirty, thank you very much.

ALLISON. *(Changing subject.)* Jack, why don't you walk us
through all of this…*deliciousness.*

JACK. I will when *all* the guests arrive.

FREYA. He better arrive.

JACK. I'm off to puff my pastry.
(*To* **ALLISON**.) Can I borrow you?

> (**JACK** *and* **ALLISON** *head off to the kitchen.*)

ALLISON. I'll get you that catalogue.

> (*A moment.* **FREYA** *helps herself to another sample.*)

FREYA. (*Shouting offstage.*) Hey. What's this thing with all the fennel?

JACK. (*Offstage. Duh!*) Uh…fennel.

> (*She tries it. More deliciousness.*)

> (*Now the doorbell rings.*)

FREYA. Finally! (*Shouting offstage.*) Todd's here. I'll get it.

> (**FREYA** *goes off. For a moment the stage is completely empty.*)

> (*Then we hear the murmuring of voices coming back down the hallway toward the stage.*)

> (**FREYA** *appears, escorting* **DAVID NATHAN BRIGHT** *into the room. He's in beautiful casual attire, his overcoat and hair wet from the rain. He has an impressive bouquet of flowers and a bottle of wine in a wooden case.*)

FREYA. (*Shouts offstage.*) Allison. Allison!
You have a visitor.

ALLISON. (*Offstage.*) What?

FREYA. A surprise visitor.

ALLISON. (*Offstage.*) Oh hi Todd! There's wine or – you probably want beer instead, yeah?

JACK. (*Offstage.*) Hey, shit face! I'll be right out. Grab some chorizo before Freya inhales it all.

> (**FREYA** *smiles at* **DAVID NATHAN BRIGHT**.)

FREYA. (*Shouts offstage.*) No. It's…a Mr. Bright –?

D.N.B. David's fine.

FREYA. – It's David?

(*Beat.* **ALLISON** *slowly emerges from the kitchen, surprised, with a bottle of Stella in one hand.*)

ALLISON. Hi.

D.N.B. Hello.

ALLISON. Hi.

D.N.B. I didn't call ahead.

I hope that's all right.

ALLISON. Of course. No, yeah.

Hi.

D.N.B. My plans changed, somewhat.

ALLISON. That's great – I don't mean that's great, I mean that's great for us – I mean.

D.N.B. Sorry for the intrusion. I won't stay long, I'm meeting a friend – I just wanted to –

ALLISON. No, please, this is great. Actually –

(*Shouting offstage.*) Jack?

I'm really happy you came.

I wasn't sure if you got my message.

D.N.B. (*A little laugh.*) Yes. I did.

ALLISON. Sorry about that.

(*She waits, nervously.* **FREYA** *looks at her expectantly.*)

Oh. This is Freya.

D.N.B. Yes, we –

FREYA. At the door.

D.N.B. Lovely to meet you. Again.

FREYA. Can I fix you a drink?

D.N.B. I'm not staying long.

ALLISON. (*Shouting offstage.*) Jack honey??

(*Offstage, it suddenly sounds like* **JACK** *may have grabbed a hot pan.*)

Can you come out here? Sweetheart?

(A beat. Then, from the kitchen, **JACK** *enters, carrying a hot platter, wearing brightly-colored oven mitts. He stops dead in his tracks when he sees* **DAVID NATHAN BRIGHT**, *trying to assess the unexpected situation at hand.)*

JACK. Burned myself.

D.N.B. You're Jack.

JACK. I'm Jack.

D.N.B. Hi Jack.

*(***JACK*** looks at* **ALLISON**.*)*

ALLISON. This is… David Nathan Bright.

*(***JACK*** puts the platter down and takes a step toward* **DAVID NATHAN BRIGHT**. *He extends his hand to shake* **DAVID NATHAN BRIGHT**'*s, still wearing the oven mitt.)*

JACK. Nice to meet you. Finally.

ALLISON. *(Re: mitt.)* Honey?

*(***JACK*** realizes his faux pas and takes off the mitt.)*

(They shake hands. **JACK** *winces slightly.)*

D.N.B. Are you all right?

JACK. Really burned myself.

(Beat.)

D.N.B. I was in the neighborhood.
I just wanted to drop these off.

ALLISON. Oh, you *really* shouldn't have.

FREYA. You brought presents.

D.N.B. It's nothing.

FREYA. It violates the pact.

D.N.B. Excuse me?

ALLISON. – Thank you, David.

D.N.B. I got your lovely card. That was very sweet. You're not the only one with a mother who valued etiquette. I wanted to return the favor. So: happy birthday.

FREYA. There's no birthday here, no sir.

JACK. Nope.

> (**DAVID NATHAN BRIGHT** *looks at* **FREYA** *and* **JACK.**)

D.N.B. Oh. I was under the impression –

FREYA.	**JACK.**
It's just a "get-together."	No. This is a "get-together." Sort of a work thing.

ALLISON. *(Embarrassed, covering.)* – Well, it's all a very low-key, casual kind of thing anyway, so… don't worry about it.

> (**ALLISON** *briefly exits to set aside the flowers.*)

D.N.B. And here's something for the chef.

> (*He hands* **JACK** *the wine case.* **JACK** *takes out the bottle.* **FREYA** *is eyeballing the whole thing.*)

Didn't know what you were preparing for your guests. I hope this will suffice.

> (**JACK** *doesn't quite know what to say.*)

JACK. Oh, this is, um…thanks.

D.N.B. Now if you'll excuse me, I must get going.

> (**DAVID NATHAN BRIGHT** *starts to leave.* **ALLISON** *runs back on.* **JACK** *and* **FREYA** *almost simultaneously impede his departure.*)

JACK. No, stay! Could you…?

> *(Simultaneously.)*

FREYA. You can't leave.

> *(Simultaneously.)*

ALLISON. No, no, don't go! *Please.*

D.N.B. I really can't. I have reservations.

JACK. Can you cancel them?

D.N.B. Not easily.

JACK. It's very important to me that you stay.
   And enjoy our hospitality.

D.N.B. I really don't like to intrude.

ALLISON. You're not – please – just for a drink?

D.N.B. Perhaps I could stay…a little while.
   Are you quite certain?

FREYA.   JACK.
   Quite.   Quite.

          (**ALLISON** *looks at* **FREYA**; **FREYA** *shrugs.*)

D.N.B. Then could I impose upon you? The rain caught me
   by surprise.

ALLISON. (*Blurts out.*) Umbrella!

          (*They all look at* **ALLISON**, *slightly thrown by the
          non sequitur.*)

D.N.B. Is there a bathroom…?

JACK. Follow me.

          (**JACK** *leads* **DAVID NATHAN BRIGHT** *offstage.*
          FREYA *rushes over to inspect the bottle of wine he
          brought.*)

FREYA. Oh my god!
   Who is he?

ALLISON. No one.

FREYA. This is an *expensive* bottle of wine.

ALLISON. How expensive?

FREYA. Like a month's salary expensive.
   Like *two* month's salary.

ALLISON. – Let me see that.

          (**ALLISON** *grabs the bottle from* **FREYA** *and inspects
          the label.*)

FREYA. I'm not kidding. Who is he?
   Someone you work with?
   Is he a friend?
   How come I've never met him?

He's very *distinguished.*

What does he do?

What's his name? David Something-Something…?

ALLISON. David Nathan Bright.

He's not even really my friend.

FREYA. Then who is he?

ALLISON. He's just this guy…

FREYA. This guy?

ALLISON. You know –

FREYA. No, what?

ALLISON. – this guy who –

FREYA. Al?

ALLISON. This guy who…bought my lunch.

(*JACK returns to the stage. Awkwardness.*)

JACK. Okay. You okay?

ALLISON. Uh-huh.

JACK. Everyone good?

FREYA. Uh-huh.

JACK. Need more wine?

ALLISON. Uh-huh.

(*Simultaneously.*)

FREYA. Uh-huh.

JACK. I'll get more wine.

(*He exits again.*)

FREYA. Come on, I'm dying.

ALLISON. (*Rattles off the bullet points.*) The day we had lunch. I couldn't find my wallet. You had to run. Jack was unreachable. David came to my assistance.

FREYA. "David came to my assistance."

ALLISON. What?

FREYA. Just: the way you said that.

He "came to my assistance."

ALLISON. That's what he did.

FREYA. What does he want?

ALLISON. He doesn't want anything. I think he's just a nice guy –

FREYA. – Do you? A nice guy?

ALLISON. I think so, yeah –

FREYA. – A "nice guy."

ALLISON. Stop putting "quotes" around everything.

FREYA. What are you *not* telling me?

ALLISON. That's what Jack said. He's a guy I just met, a casual – not even acquaintance.

FREYA. A casual acquaintance doesn't bring a $6,000 bottle of wine to a dinner party.

ALLISON. Six *thou* –?

FREYA. That's right. That's why *L'Odyssée* wants me. I know my wine.

ALLISON. That's insane. I am not letting him open that bottle.

FREYA. Well, you can't, can you? Not when Jack's been saving *his* bottle for this "special occasion."

ALLISON. Okay, enough with the "quotes."

FREYA. Happy birthday? How come he's the only one allowed to acknowledge –

ALLISON. That was a simple misunderstanding.

FREYA. If I'd come with a gift would that have been a simple misunderstanding?

ALLISON. You *didn't* come with a gift.

FREYA. I *KNOW*!! And now I feel like an *asshole* – thank you very much – I *knew* this was going to happen. I thought we had a pact.

ALLISON. We *do* have a pact.

FREYA. But David Something-Something came with a gift.

ALLISON. David Nathan Bright.

FREYA. "David Nathan Bright."

ALLISON. You're *doing* it again.

FREYA. Why does he get to violate the pact? How did he

even *know* it was your birthday? *(Quick beat.)* And where the hell is my husband?

ALLISON. Are you pissed off at Todd? Or me?

FREYA. I'm not pissed off, I'm…*something else.*

ALLISON. *(Jumping on this.)* Oh, my god! That's what Jack said. He said *he* was "something else." When I told him about this guy who bought my lunch, he said he was feeling "something else." But that "something else" feels decidedly like "pissed off."

He bought my lunch. That's all. It was an act of generosity, okay, and *now* –

FREYA. You're in his debt.

ALLISON. I'm not in his debt. Why do you say that? I'm not in his debt.

FREYA. *(Grabs the bottle.)* Six thousand dollars.

ALLISON. *(Grabs it back.)* Which we are not opening.

FREYA. It was a gift.

For your *birthday.*

You can't *not* open it.

ALLISON. Then I'll give it back.

FREYA. *Rude!*

ALLISON. Or – Hold onto it I guess.

FREYA. And *re-gift* it?

ALLISON. What?

FREYA. Never mind.

> *(Brief pause.)*

The protocol? In a situation like this? The protocol – I think – a bottle like that is intended to be opened at the event to which it is brought.

ALLISON. That's the protocol?

FREYA. I don't know! – No one ever gave me a $6,000 bottle of wine!

ALLISON. It's too much.

FREYA. Well you're fucked. You can't give it back, you can't decline. What are you going to do?

> *(There is a brief silence, neither one of them knowing what to say next. Then* **FREYA** *exhales audibly, levelling* **ALLISON** *with a look.)*

FREYA. *(Cont.)* I have to ask… Are you fucking him?

ALLISON. *What?*

FREYA. I had to ask!

ALLISON. Was there a gun to your head?

FREYA. Come on: are you fucking David Something-Something?

ALLISON. Why can't anyone remember his name? It's *David… Nathan… Bright.*

FREYA. Are you sleeping with this David Nathan Bright? A man gives you a lavish gift like that, it's a reasonable assumption.

ALLISON. No, Freya – I am not… *(Sotto voce.) sleeping with him!*

I should have kept my mouth shut.

I should never have told Jack.

Should never have invited him. But I felt –

FREYA. *(With inexplicable hostility.)* Obligated?

ALLISON. Why is everyone angry?

FREYA. I'm not angry.

I would tell you if I was angry. Believe me.

It's one of the things I'm working on with Zoe.

ALLISON. Who's Zoe?

FREYA. *Owning* my feelings.

ALLISON. Who's Zoe, Freya?

FREYA. But I don't *own!* That's what Zoe said: I don't own my feelings, I *rent.*

ALLISON. *Who's Zoe??*

FREYA. Our therapist – I told you this.

ALLISON. You and Todd –?

FREYA. – Yeah, I told you this.

ALLISON. No you didn't, Freya. You said you were okay. At lunch you told me everything was okay.

FREYA. It is okay.

ALLISON. You're in therapy.

FREYA. Isn't everyone? Aren't you?

ALLISON. No.

FREYA. Oh. I thought – You're not in therapy?

ALLISON. What?

FREYA. Because –

Jack said –

ALLISON. What did Jack say?

Freya.

What are you – what did he say?

*(**FREYA** doesn't answer.)*

(Calling offstage.) Jack!!

*(Now, just as **JACK** returns to the stage with a plate of puff pastries, from down the hallway we hear someone knocking loudly and pushing through the front door.)*

TODD. *(Offstage.)* Guys?

Hey, guys. Sorry I'm late.

(We hear something crash out in the hallway.)

FREYA. Todd?

TODD. *(Offstage.)* Sorry, I'll buy you another one of those.

JACK. You made it.

*(**TODD** appears from the hallway, briefcase in one hand, holding one of those colorful, clear plastic umbrellas in the other.)*

TODD. *(To **JACK**.)* Hey, dick wad!

JACK. Hi, shit face!

(They embrace, clumsily.)

*(It's immediately clear **TODD**'s had too much to drink. He sways unsteadily on his feet.)*

FREYA. What took you so long?

TODD. Traffic. Weather. Combo of traffic and weather.

JACK. Nice umbrella.

TODD. The wife's.

> (**TODD** *extends the umbrella to* **FREYA.**)

JACK. No it's not. (**JACK** *holds out the umbrella he found in Scene Three to* **FREYA.***) This* is the wife's.

FREYA. Not it's not.

JACK. Then whose is it?

> (**DAVID NATHAN BRIGHT** *has returned from the bathroom.*)

D.N.B. It's Allison's.

JACK. *(To* **ALLISON.***)* This is yours?

ALLISON. No it's not.

> (**TODD** *looks oddly at the umbrella he's holding.*)

TODD. Then whose is this? *(Re:* **DAVID NATHAN BRIGHT.***)* And who is *that?*

ALLISON. I don't want it – please, take it back!

D.N.B. You must be Todd.

> (**DAVID NATHAN BRIGHT** *extends a hand to shake, but* **TODD***'s looking pale; maybe a little suppressed burp.*)

Are you all right?

FREYA. Todd – meet David Nathan Bright.

> (**TODD** *vomits on* **DAVID NATHAN BRIGHT.***)
>
> *(Snap to black.)*
>
> *(Intermission.)*

ACT TWO

Scene Seven

*(We've been deposited right back at the end of the
first act, only a few minutes later. **FREYA** is on
her hands and knees with a bucket, bottle of spray
cleaner, and sponge, cleaning up the mess left on
the floor by her husband. She wears rubber dish
gloves. **ALLISON** is off down the hallway; we hear
her sweeping up broken glass. Mid-conversation:)*

FREYA. I'm gonna kill him.

ALLISON. *(Offstage.)* No you're not.

FREYA. I'm going to kill him.

ALLISON. *(Offstage.)* Freya.

FREYA. I am literally going to kill that man.

> *(**ALLISON** enters carrying a dustpan filled with
> the remnants of whatever **TODD** destroyed on his
> entrance.)*

ALLISON. Don't worry about it.

FREYA. He shows up late.

Shows up utterly plastered.

He annihilates your *priceless* sculpture –

ALLISON. From Pier 1.

FREYA. – barfs on your new best friend.

ALLISON. He's not my best friend.

FREYA. Barfs on what's-his-face.

> *(**ALLISON** sighs.)*

ALLISON. Please don't make a scene. When Todd comes

out, can we all just – can we have a pleasant evening? Can you do that for me?

I know you're angry with me…

> (*She starts to go off toward the kitchen with the dustpan.*)

FREYA. Yes… I think I am.

> (**ALLISON** *turns back with keen interest.*)

ALLISON. Do you know why? Can you help me understand *why?*

FREYA. How should *I* know?

ALLISON. Jack's angry too.

He's pretending he's not.

But I can tell.

(*A confession.*) We had angry sex.

FREYA. (*It's a Cosmo moment, her interest piqued.*) You did?

ALLISON. We did.

FREYA. How was it?

ALLISON. Pretty good, actually.

> (**JACK** *returns to the stage.*)

JACK. Well, as you can imagine, he's a little embarrassed.

ALLISON. Why is he embarrassed?

JACK. *Hello!* He just threw up on one of our guests.

ALLISON. I meant David Nathan Bright.

JACK. Oh he's um…changing… I put out some clothes. Todd's taking a shower. He's going to lie down for a bit.

ALLISON. Jack? Are you still angry?

JACK. No – what? No – what? No.

> (**JACK** *exits, taking the dustpan and brush right from* **ALLISON**'s *hands.*)

ALLISON. He's angry.

FREYA. He *should* be angry. He has more of a right to be angry than I do, and I'm pretty angry. (*Before* **ALLISON** *can protest,* **FREYA** *raises a hand.*) Don't ask me why!!

There's something odd about that man.

ALLISON. You just met him.

FREYA. Don't *you* think he's odd?

ALLISON. I can't place my finger on it.

He's kind.

He's elegant.

He's…*non-threatening*.

FREYA. Is he gay? (**ALLISON** *glares at her.*) – What? He was very well-dressed.

ALLISON. I don't know if he's gay.

FREYA. Ask him.

ALLISON. What?

FREYA. Ask him…when he comes out of that bedroom, ask the guy.

ALLISON. I am not going to ask him if –

FREYA. It could help us divine his agenda.

ALLISON. He doesn't have an agenda, Freya.

FREYA. I guess we'll find out, won't we?

(*Now, from offstage, we hear* **DAVID NATHAN BRIGHT** *calling from the bedroom area.*)

D.N.B. (*Offstage.*) I just left my shirt in the tub, is that okay?

ALLISON. (*Calling offstage.*) Okay!

FREYA. I have a bad feeling: this is not going to end well.

ALLISON. Don't make a scene!

(**DAVID NATHAN BRIGHT** *returns to the stage. He is wearing one of* **JACK***'s sweaters and a t-shirt;* **JACK** *comes in carrying a tray of food.*)

D.N.B. I love that thing hanging in your bathroom.

ALLISON. You can have it!

D.N.B. What?

ALLISON. (*Starts to run out.*) – Stay put, I'll go grab it.

D.N.B. No I don't want it, I was just admiring it.

ALLISON. Oh. Okay. You sure?

D.N.B. Yes, I'm quite sure.

FREYA. Can I have it?

ALLISON. Please sit down. Everyone.

> (**DAVID NATHAN BRIGHT** *and* **ALLISON** *sit;* **FREYA** *does not. There is a moment; everyone looking quietly at one another.* **FREYA** *breaks the silence.*)

FREYA. David, is it okay if I call you David? Can I just take a moment to say how… *mortified* is the word. Todd's been under a lot of pressure at work. *(She stops herself.)* Why am I making excuses? He vomited on you.

D.N.B. I'm actually fine. Don't fuss over me. I'm all grown up.

FREYA. *(Like a bloodhound.)* Yeah, how old are you?

D.N.B. Pardon?

ALLISON. Okay, drinks, who wants a drink? *(Quickly, offstage to* **JACK***.)* Jack, sweetie.

> (**JACK** *briefly returns to the room.*)

JACK. Yeah?

ALLISON. Drinks?

JACK. Yeah.

D.N.B. *(To* **JACK***.)* Thanks for the loaner by the way.

JACK. Yeah, yeah.

> (**JACK** *runs off for more glasses.*)

ALLISON. It looks a little tight.

D.N.B. I swim.

FREYA. What does that mean?

D.N.B. I go swimming. In a pool –?

FREYA. *(Like she's discovered a new unknown species.)* Interesting.

D.N.B. – so I have a problem, sometimes, getting things to fit around the shoulders. As a consequence, I have to get my shirts made.

FREYA. *(Trying to get a read on him, but can't.)* Huh.

D.N.B. This wonderful guy – his grandfather, actually – came over from Italy in… I always screw up the story – but *his* family's made shirts for all the men in *my* family for years.

FREYA. There's more of you?

D.N.B. Sorry?

FREYA. Big family, you say? Are you Catholic?

D.N.B. *(A little confused by the question.)* No. Some of my friends get their shirts done there too. He's a perfectionist, a true artisan, which is impossible to find these days.

FREYA. Do you have a lot of friends? Who wear shirts?

ALLISON. *(Hoping to cover the absurdity of the question.)* Drink, Freya?

D.N.B. You know, I've never really thought about it, in that way.

(**JACK** *returns with glasses, etc.*)

JACK. I hope you guys are hungry. We should… *(Re: the food.)* …tuck in.

ALLISON. – Yes –!

D.N.B. Allison said you knew your way around a kitchen, but I had no idea I was dining with an accomplished restaurateur.

JACK. Try it first before you shovel on the praise.

ALLISON. Oh it looks amazing, babe. Freya, you should eat something.

JACK. And I'm not a restaurateur yet, just a lowly chef. *(He laughs at his own joke.)* Who knows with these investors, right, a fickle bunch… moment to moment, a downturn in the market and it all vaporizes.

ALLISON. *(A little surprised.)* We're officially talking about this?

JACK. *(Equally surprised; smiles.)* I guess we're officially talking about this.

ALLISON. Jack's close to a commitment from a major

investor.

D.N.B. So I gather. *(To* **JACK.***)* Think it's a brilliant concept, by-the-way. I promise to become a regular.

JACK. You haven't tasted a thing yet. Grab a plate.

D.N.B. It all looks fabulous.

JACK. Everyone, just dig in.

> *(Everyone heads for the table, except* **FREYA,** *who still has her sights on* **DAVID NATHAN BRIGHT***, watching his every move and drinking more wine than is perhaps good for her.)*

ALLISON. Freya, you're not eating?

FREYA. I'm drinking. And thinking.

> *(She turns toward* **DAVID NATHAN BRIGHT***, preparing a second salvo.)*

Your shirt. I'll have it dry cleaned, and delivered to – do you live nearby?

D.N.B. Not particularly.

FREYA. ...Where exactly *do* you live?

D.N.B. Don't worry about it. I have a dozen of the same shirt.

ALLISON. What are you drinking, David?

D.N.B. Why don't we open my bottle?

JACK. Lovely.

> *(***JACK** *grabs it and the wine key.* **ALLISON** *quickly dashes over and grabs the bottle from* **JACK***'s hand, shaking her head.)*

ALLISON. *(Louder than she thought.)* WHY??

> *(***JACK** *and* **DAVID NATHAN BRIGHT** *look at her.)*

Why...don't we save that one for later?

> *(***JACK** *proceeds to go round filling up everyone's glass from another open bottle.)*

(Re: the tapas.) Jack why don't you walk us through this?

> *(They all gather round for* **JACK***'s presentation.)*

JACK. Okay.
Salted cod with cherry tomato salad.
Venison mousse and toast points.
This: a veggie paella topped with goat's cheese.
Some croquetas: wild mushroom here, and spiced sausage there.
Freya can vouch for the squid, and the fennel.
Yeah: pretty simple.

ALLISON. *(Her little joke.)* We eat like this every day.

> (**DAVID NATHAN BRIGHT** *laughs, enjoying himself.*)

JACK. The Rioja's great with the venison.

D.N.B. *(His mouth full of something.)* Jack, Jack, this is...

JACK. And I'd suggest this little white number to go with the sausage.

D.N.B. Where are my manners? Napkin, please.

> (**ALLISON** *passes a napkin.*)

ALLISON. There you are.

> (**JACK** *hands* **DAVID NATHAN BRIGHT** *a small side dish.*)

JACK. Dip it in the truffled honey.
And seriously, guys, any criticism, don't hold back. I could use the feedback.

ALLISON. *(Her mouth full of something.)* Cribicism?

JACK. This is what I'm letting the investors taste next week, so if there's room for improvement...

D.N.B. The only improvement I can see is if you'd invited fewer guests, there'd be more for me.

> (**JACK** *and* **ALLISON** *share a laugh.*)

JACK. Well, thank you for the compliment. It means a lot.

D.N.B. You're welcome.

JACK. No. Actually, David...
I'm glad that you came, so we could – so I could...
thank you properly.

(*Everyone is looking at* **DAVID NATHAN BRIGHT**.)

D.N.B. Please. There's no need.

JACK. Yes, there is.

You were kind enough to buy a meal for my fiancée.

(**DAVID NATHAN BRIGHT** *looks over at* **ALLISON**. **FREYA** *is studying all this intensely.*)

And now, I'm happy to prepare one for you.

D.N.B. And what an extraordinary meal it is.

(*A beat, then:*)

JACK. So, we're even.

Right?

D.N.B. Even?

JACK. I mean: as the saying goes.

(*There is a silence that* **DAVID NATHAN BRIGHT** *finally breaks.*)

D.N.B. Do you have a name for it yet?

The restaurant?

JACK. Not yet.

ALLISON. It'll come to him.

D.N.B. I'm sure it will.

JACK. It will.

(**FREYA** *is helping herself to more wine. She scooches over and pats the seat, making room for him to sit beside her.*)

FREYA. So, David…

I'm curious…

What do you do?

D.N.B. Sorry?

FREYA. Job-wise?

D.N.B. Well, you know…this and that.

FREYA. No, what does that mean?

I don't know what that means.

Are you in the service industry yourself, or –?

D.N.B. Funnily enough, I've always wanted to have a restaurant.

JACK. Really?

D.N.B. Always a secret dream of mine. But – you know – I lack the one key ingredient for any successful restaurant.

FREYA. And what's that?

D.N.B. Competence. I don't know the first thing about it.

> (**JACK** *is enjoying himself now, having apparently set the scales even once again.*)

Wouldn't have a clue where to begin. That's me. All passion, no talent.

ALLISON. I'm sure that's not true.

D.N.B. In most things. Sadly, it is.
I do, however, dine at a lot of them: restaurants… So, I suppose one could say, I'm living a vicarious life. Through people like yourself, Jack. People with the real talent.

FREYA. To get back to my original question: what do you do? If you don't mind.

ALLISON. Freya, can I fix you a plate?

FREYA. I'm fine.

> (**FREYA** *extends an empty wine glass to* **ALLISON**, *who reluctantly refills it.*)

David?

D.N.B. Oh, it's rather boring.

FREYA. I'm a terrific listener.

D.N.B. Well. I – you sure you want to know –?

FREYA. Pins and needles!

D.N.B. Well…

FREYA. Uh-huh?

D.N.B. I'm heavily involved in the arts.

ALLISON. I didn't know that.

FREYA. So you're an artist?

D.N.B. Not exactly, no. I'm passionate about the arts. So I serve on a number of boards. Art galleries, mostly, museums, several theaters, the Opera.

JACK. And what exactly do...?

D.N.B. You could say I serve in an advisory capacity.

FREYA. You give them money?

D.N.B. Well, certainly...but that's a very small part of it. I build alliances. With like-minded individuals. Business leaders, corporations, and –

FREYA. Ask *them* to give money.

D.N.B. You see this is what I'm *trying* to inculcate in these circles: the idea that – you see, it's more than that, it's much more – it *has* to be more than simply giv –

FREYA. What's the other part?

D.N.B. Pardon?

FREYA. You said giving money was a small part of what you do. What's the other part? The big part? That's what I'd like to know.

ALLISON. Can we talk about something else? David doesn't have much time –

D.N.B. You're right.

ALLISON. – he's barely touched his food.

D.N.B. I really should think about going. But Jack, this is truly spectacular.

JACK. Before you go, David, I'd like to propose a toast.

> (**JACK** *grabs the bottle of wine he's been saving for this occasion.*)

ALLISON. Shouldn't we wait? For Todd?

JACK. Oh. Okay. I suppose you're right. *(He puts the bottle back.)* Can you stay a little longer, David? Ten minutes.

D.N.B. I'll need to make a quick call. *(He takes out his phone.)* Tell someone I'm running late. I'm not getting great reception here, can I...?

ALLISON. Yeah, this building's weird. There's a little balcony off the kitchen...

JACK. …If you hug the wall by the wine rack. That's the sweet spot.

 (**DAVID** *exits toward the kitchen.*)

ALLISON. What's the matter with you?

FREYA. What? I'm inquisitive.

ALLISON. Oh, I could think of another word!

 (**TODD** *now emerges from the bedroom. He is disheveled, but looks a far sight better than when he first arrived. He's got a kind of buoyant second-wind look about him.*)

TODD. Hey.

JACK. Hey.

ALLISON. You feeling better?

TODD. What I miss?

JACK. Hungry?

TODD. In a bit.

FREYA. Where were you?

TODD. In a bar.

FREYA. *That's* obvious.

ALLISON. Freya – *please* – let's all make an effort to keep this evening bright?

 (**TODD** *and* **FREYA** *look at one another.* **ALLISON** *crosses to* **TODD** *and gives him a hug.*)

Nice to see you, stranger.

TODD. *(Re: his entrance earlier.)* Sorry about your *thing*.

ALLISON. I'm just glad you're here.

(To **FREYA.***)* Don't you have some important news for Todd?

TODD. I got news for you too.

FREYA. You go first.

TODD. I quit.

FREYA.	**ALLISON.**
What?	What?

TODD. Fucking Lexus!

> (**ALLISON** *inhales and appears to be holding her breath.* **FREYA** *involuntarily sits on the couch.*)

FREYA. Now *I'm* going to be sick.

JACK. *Why,* why did you quit?

TODD. They were going to fire me. Didn't want to give them the satisfaction.

JACK. Jesus! Todd. What can we do? You need anything?

TODD. Some wine?

FREYA. Are you kidding me?

TODD. My nerves are on edge, all right?

> (*He dribbles the remainder of a bottle into a glass for himself.*)

FREYA. Why were you so late? Where did you go? Did you get any of my texts?

TODD. I thought about going to see Zoe.

JACK. Who's Zoe –?

ALLISON. – Jack.

TODD. But then I made other plans.

FREYA. What other plans?

TODD. Thought I'd get shit-faced instead. You know, deal with my problems in a responsible way.

JACK. *(Handing him a fresh glass.)* What happened, man? How did you quit?

TODD. Very… *vocally*…as I recall.
Used some choice words in describing the sales manager's wife. And daughter.

JACK. *Fuck!*

TODD. That was one of the words.

> (*He swallows some wine, and looks at all the food.*)

Wow! This looks great. Even slightly nauseous.

JACK. Thanks – might use that in the PR: "Great food: even when slightly nauseous."

(**TODD**'s *gaining back his appetite and starts to circle the table.*)

Eat whatever; there's no cilantro.

(**TODD** *levels a look at* **FREYA**.)

TODD. Thank you, Jack! Is that chorizo?

(**TODD** *helps himself to a nibble. He looks over at* **FREYA**.)

So…what was *your* news?

What did you wish to impart, dearest?

FREYA. *(Flatly.)* I made an offer on a house.

TODD. Well. Isn't that *ironical?*

JACK. You'll work things out.

TODD. Will we? I love when people say that: "We'll work things out." It's a reflex. What you say when you realize you have no fucking clue how to extricate yourself from the shit circumstance you find yourself in, and, as it turns out, there is no way to *work things out!* It's why I *didn't* go to Zoe. I knew it would be the first dumb thing out of her mouth.

JACK. Who is Zoe?

FREYA. Can you get your job back?

TODD. I don't want the damned thing.

ALLISON. Let's not do this while David's here –

TODD. – Who's David?

FREYA. David Nathan Bright.

TODD. I know that name. Is he an actor –?

ALLISON. – No –

TODD. – I thought only actors had three names.

JACK. Or people who shoot presidents.

FREYA. Allison's new buddy.

TODD. Never met him.

JACK. The guy you puked on?

TODD. *(That rings a bell.)* Oh. I did that, huh?

(**DAVID NATHAN BRIGHT** *returns to the room, pocketing his cell phone.*)

D.N.B. I'm all yours for a bit longer. *(To* **TODD**.) Hi Todd. I'm David. We met earlier.

TODD. The guy I puked on?

D.N.B. Don't worry about it.

TODD. I wasn't.

(**ALLISON** *and* **JACK** *are horrified, but* **DAVID NATHAN BRIGHT** *finds* **TODD**'s *comment to be rather charming and funny.* **JACK** *hands* **DAVID NATHAN BRIGHT** *back his glass.*)

D.N.B. Well then: now it's my turn to be curious. How do you all know each other?

FREYA. From college.

ALLISON. *(Re:* **FREYA**.) We were roommates.

FREYA. We have a *backstory*. Do *you* have a backstory?

(**ALLISON** *tries to leap right over* **FREYA**'s *comment.*)

ALLISON. And Jack and Todd were… *(To* **TODD**.)…well, what were you…?

TODD.	**JACK.**
(Simultaneously with **JACK**.)	Bosom buddies.
Rivals.	

(*Beat.*)

JACK. I think the technical term is "drunks."

(**TODD** *chuckles into his wine glass.*)

FREYA. Some things never change.

TODD. *(Raises his glass.)* Cheers!

D.N.B. And that's where you and Jack first…?

ALLISON. I was an Art major, *briefly*…

D.N.B. Really?

ALLISON. And then a Philosophy major… I *dabbled*… had dreams of becoming a poet…*ultimately*, I think I majored in *indecision.*

> (**TODD** *likes this.*)

…And Jack was…

D.N.B. Do you still write?

ALLISON. God no, gave that up a long time ago. Had to get serious, you know? And Jack…

> (*The mood is now very easy, with* **FREYA,** *in spite of herself, softening a little to enjoy* **ALLISON***'s reminiscence.*)

JACK. – Jack was in culinary school. Well, I dropped out of college to go to culinary school, *but* I checked out this creative writing class when I learned Allison had signed up.

TODD. The academically sanctioned version of stalking. *(They all laugh.)*

FREYA. You've really opened up a can of worms now, David, they just loooooove talking about this shit.

JACK. We do. We love talking about this shit.

ALLISON. And Jack – well, he –

JACK. I made her a cake.

D.N.B. A cake?

ALLISON. He did.

JACK. A three-tiered chocolate cake.

ALLISON. And on it he'd written, in blue icing, he'd written –

JACK. "I do not love you except because I love you."

> (**ALLISON** *and* **JACK** *look at one another and smile.* **DAVID NATHAN BRIGHT** *also adds an appreciative laugh.* **FREYA** *and* **TODD** *feel left out of the joke.*)

FREYA. They do this, they do this all the time – *(She looks to* **TODD** *for confirmation.)* – right? I've never asked you guys…what the hell are you talking about?

D.N.B. *(Simply.)* It's Neruda.

ALLISON. Yes.

FREYA. What?

JACK. Pablo Neruda.

D.N.B. "I do not love you, except because I love you;
　　I go from loving to not loving you,
　　From waiting to not waiting for you
　　My heart moves from the cold into the fire."*

> *(**ALLISON** offers a little applause.)*

JACK. Well done.

ALLISON. It's been our little joke for years.

FREYA. I don't get it. Why don't I know this?

JACK. I didn't do my homework –

TODD. That sounds like you.

JACK. – always late to class, I just knew Allison loved Neruda and thought it would be cool to scrawl this quote in icing across the cake I made for her birthday.

> *(**JACK** has said this before he is even aware of what he's done. He now looks guiltily at **ALLISON**.)*

I'm sorry. I mean –

ALLISON. *(She's willing to overlook the fault.)* He didn't realize the poem was about someone who's in a one-sided love affair. They give all their love to someone who can't return it.

> *(This now lands in the room much harder than she intended, so she is compelled to go on. **FREYA** glances over at **TODD**. He's aware that she's looking at him, but cannot return the look.)*

When I saw the cake I burst out laughing. But it was also the sweetest thing anyone had ever done for me. So…anyway.

D.N.B. That's a wonderful story.

---

* From 100 LOVE SONNETS: CIEN SONETOS DE AMOR by Pablo Neruda, translated by Stephen Tapscott, Copyright © Pablo Neruda 1959 and Fundacion Pablo Neruda, Copyright © 1986 by the University of Texas Press. By permission of the University of Texas Press.

JACK. A little syrupy.

D.N.B. When you love someone…*deeply*… I think syrupy is permitted.

> *(A beat, then:)*

And you? Freya, you and Todd? How did you two meet?

TODD. This'll be good.

> *(She glances at **TODD**, tolerating him much more than she expects to.)*

FREYA. *(Deadpan.)* He worked at a car dealership.

I went to buy a car.

We took a test drive.

We ended up having sex.

> *(There is a moment here, where no one is quite sure how to take this…but then the absurd contrast to **ALLISON**'s heartfelt story releases the tension all round. Laughter.)*

TODD. That sounds about right.

D.N.B. What kind of car was it?

FREYA. I can't remember. I didn't buy it.

TODD. *Think!!*

FREYA. Some kinda Ford.

D.N.B. *(Incredulous.)* You didn't buy it?

> *(The laughter grows. **ALLISON** hugs and kisses **FREYA**.)*

FREYA. *What?* He wouldn't give me a deal, so, fuck it!

ALLISON. Freya, I love you.

FREYA. What??

> *(They are still laughing. **FREYA**'s not sure why.)*

It was a hatchback. What?

D.N.B. Well, I have to say, I think that's the most *unique*…

> *(But **ALLISON**'s been swept up in the nostalgia of the last few minutes and doesn't even think about what she now asks:)*

ALLISON. And what about you, David?

Is there a lady in your life?

Someone special?

Come on, we've all been dragging out our skeletons.

> *(Silence.)*
>
> *(***DAVID NATHAN BRIGHT*** slowly puts down his plate.)*
>
> *(He stands.)*
>
> *(He smiles.)*
>
> *(He gives a little formal half-bow.)*

D.N.B. This has been lovely.

Very kind of you to invite me in.

I think perhaps I should be going now.

I'm meeting an old friend who is only briefly in town on business.

ALLISON. Yes. Okay. Completely understand. Sorry we sidetracked you.

D.N.B. No, it was lovely, really.

JACK. Can I send you home with something? *(He gestures to the table of delectable food.)*

D.N.B. Thank you, no. It was wonderful getting to meet you all and… Jack, I'm very impressed. *(***JACK*** starts to protest.)* I dine at many fine restaurants, and this is on par, no… this *exceeds*, far and away, much of what I've tasted the world over. I'm very optimistic for your future. Good luck picking out a name. I know people in advertising if you need help in that department, don't hesitate to ask.

JACK. You've been more than helpful already.

D.N.B. *(Suddenly realizing he's wearing ***JACK****'s clothes.)* I will have this returned.

JACK. Cool.

> *(***ALLISON*** escorts ***DAVID NATHAN BRIGHT*** toward the door. The others rise to say their goodbyes. Only*

FREYA *remains seated. Just as* **DAVID NATHAN BRIGHT** *is about to leave the room…)*

FREYA. *(A real attention-getter.)* I got a new job today.

(They all look back at her.)

TODD. What?

D.N.B. Oh. Wonderful. You must be pleased.

(He starts out again, but…)

FREYA. Aren't you going to stay to congratulate me?

D.N.B. *(Awkward.)* Well…as I said –

FREYA. I mean: you came all this way to congratulate Allison.

On her birthday.

TODD.	**JACK.**
– Honey –?	Freya.

FREYA. Even though it's not her birthday.

Or is it?

I don't know.

It's weird.

(It's clear now that somewhere in the last few minutes **FREYA***'s crossed over the line from tipsy to drunk – and she is now extra-animated.)*

We've only been friends since college. But that whole birthday thing is just this big old black hole of *weirdness*.

And yet, here you are.

TODD. – Okay, Freya –

FREYA. Mr. Generosity –

Mister Man With Three Names, who's not an actor.

Bringing *gifts*.

Wishing *well*.

We're not supposed to give gifts, if you hadn't noticed.

So, why don't you stay to congratulate me – on my new job – that I *think* I got offered this morning… – but I'm not sure I got the job, not *one hunnnered puuuuuuurcent!* Because of her fucking *accent*. *(Beat.)* I *think* I got the job, I mean, I *think* I did, I deserve it… I'm totally qualified… I'm really *super-good* at what I do, which is wine. I do wine, I know wine, I sell wine – which is why I know about *your* wine, you… *dick.*

ALLISON.	**JACK.**	**TODD.**
Freya!	Freya!	Whoa!

ALLISON. Todd?

> (**ALLISON** *tries to redirect* **FREYA**'*s energy by taking her by the arm, but* **FREYA** *shrugs it off with disproportionate violence. But* **DAVID NATHAN BRIGHT** *doesn't react. He just continues.*)

D.N.B. You sell wine?

FREYA. *Interesting*, isn't it?

D.N.B. I was going to say *coincidental.* My friend – the one I'm meeting – from Paris. She's in town for that very reason.

FREYA. (*Sloppily.*) She's *innerviewing* for a wine job?

> (**DAVID** *nods.*)

Well, you can tell your Parisian pal… I've got it in the bag…the job's mine, okay? – Well, I *think* it's mine – but who knows with the French, something may have gotten lost in translation.

ALLISON. Freya I think you should –

D.N.B. Pauline's not here to get a job. She's here to hire someone for the company she owns.

> (*There is a dreadful silence as it dawns on* **FREYA** *what has just transpired.*)

FREYA. Pauline…?

(*Feeling suddenly quite small.*) Well, fuck!

> (**FREYA** *downs her entire glass of wine. But* **DAVID NATHAN BRIGHT** *suddenly changes the atmosphere in the room, as if by magic. He begins to smile, then chuckle, and then roar with laughter.*)

D.N.B. This is great! Wouldn't you say? It's fate. It obviously means something, doesn't it? I can't believe this…what a fortunate… *(He laughs.)* …Pauline. She really would appreciate the irony.

> *(There's a moment where everyone is struck by the sudden strangeness of the situation unfolding.)*

JACK. Invite her over. You're not going to make your reservations anyway. There's plenty of food.

D.N.B. You don't mind?

JACK. Invite her over.

ALLISON. Jack, maybe –

D.N.B. – Freya, you said you *thought* she offered you the job but you're not entirely sure. We could find out. Right now. Put your mind at ease. I'd be happy to do that for you.

ALLISON. *(To* **FREYA.***)* Are you okay?

FREYA. *(To* **DAVID.***)* What's wrong with you? What do you want?

D.N.B. I…should I call her?

FREYA. Why are you so nice? Why do you keep – *doing things?*

D.N.B. Look, I know how Pauline is when you meet her in a professional context, she's stiff, it's intimidating. But if you get to know her… I mean, god, I knew her when we were all walking barefoot around the south of France and she played bongos, I'm not kidding, she was the bongo player in this Algerian band. She has this playful side. You'll see. Let me call her. Let me do that for you.

FREYA. I was just incredibly insulting to you and now you want to do me a favor?

> **(DAVID NATHAN BRIGHT** *smiles and nods gleefully.)*

D.N.B. It's nothing.

> *(He takes out his phone and exits again toward the kitchen.)*

ALLISON. Isn't he something?

You're welcome, by the way.

FREYA. You're taking credit?

What the hell is the matter with you?

What the hell is the matter with *him?*

ALLISON. No, just: everyone had their doubts about David, everyone was intensely suspicious. It turns out, he's a wonderful guy. He's genuinely – nice, he's genuinely… generous.

> *(***FREYA*** scoffs.)*

FREYA. Unlike some. Little Miss Re-gifter.

> *(***FREYA*** stands and crosses to find ***TODD****'s briefcase sitting in the hallway. She pulls out the leather planner and holds it above her head triumphantly.)*

ALLISON. What?

FREYA. This. This piece of shit gift you gave me at lunch. That's what!

TODD. *(To ***FREYA****.)* Hey, you gave that to me.

FREYA. *(Viciously.)* Shut up, Todd! *(To ***ALLISON****.)* Your thoughtful good luck charm? For my interview? Except it took no thought at all, did it? You just *regurgitated* the same gift I'd bought for your husband last year.

ALLISON. Freya, you're really drunk!

FREYA. Yep, *still.* You've made such a big deal about David Nathan Bright and his munificence. I couldn't figure out why I was so angry. It just hit me. It's not *his* generosity that pisses me off, it's *your* selfishness.

JACK. Hey, now!

FREYA. Don't act like you don't know what I'm talking about, Jackie Boy! We've had our little *chats. (Back to* **ALLISON***.)* You are so fucking unbelievably stingy. You don't want to receive, you *can't* receive…because you don't like to *give.* Right? Jack am I right? And as far as I can tell it's not just *things* you withhold, not just *gifts.* It's *yourself.* Big fat chunks of *yourself.* Jack? I'm not misrepresenting, here, am I? I mean, I think what I'm saying is a direct *verbatim* quote.

ALLISON. *(Disoriented.)* Jack?

FREYA. Which is why the pair of you have been in therapy. So don't look down your nose at us like we're the only ones with problems.

(**ALLISON** *does not know what to say, except:*)

ALLISON. We're not in therapy.

JACK. I am.

(Silence.)

ALLISON. What?

JACK. I've been seeing someone.

(Maybe he shouldn't but...)

When you love someone – it's like this great big house. You get to know them room by room – I mean, you never expect to get a glimpse at *every* room. There have to be some parts withheld – I get that, I'm not a complete fool, that's only human...but with you, Al... it's not just rooms, it's whole goddamned *wings*. An entire annex of shit you just refuse to share with me.

ALLISON. *(Almost inaudibly.)* I don't like birthdays.

(There is a moment of silence, then...)

*(**TODD**'s cell phone beeps. He's received a text.)*

FREYA. Who the fuck keeps texting you?
Give me that.

(**FREYA** *wrests the cellphone from* **TODD**'s *hand. She stops dead when she reads the message.*)

Who's Kate?
Todd?
Who the hell is Kate?

TODD. *(Snatches back phone.)* You wouldn't understand.

(**DAVID NATHAN BRIGHT** *returns to the room.*)

D.N.B. She's coming – it's a quick cab ride over, so. Ten minutes, tops. She's excited to meet you again Freya.

Said you interviewed *very* well. *(He senses the temperature change in the room. He looks around.)* Is everything okay?

(A brief silence, and then…)

FREYA. Did she confirm?

D.N.B. Excuse me?

FREYA. Whether I got the job or not?

TODD. *(Laughing in spite of everything.)* Jesus Christ!

D.N.B. She's very eager to discuss things further.

FREYA. Don't be cryptic.

JACK. She'll be here soon enough.

FREYA. No. Call her back. Isn't that what you *do*, David? You *do* nice things, for people. You come to their assistance? Without…*apparently* wanting anything in return?

TODD. Are you nuts? Have you lost *all…moral…*

FREYA. I cannot *conceive* of spending the rest of the night with this *woman*, okay, if she's actually not hiring me for the job – let me remind you – that I am *more* than qualified to do!

> *(**ALLISON** is mortified. She needs to put some distance between herself and the rest of the room.)*

ALLISON. David, I am so sorry.

> *(But once again, **DAVID NATHAN BRIGHT** redirects the energy in the room.)*

D.N.B. Jack. Don't you have a toast or something?

JACK. *(Incomprehensible.)* What? Now?

D.N.B. Now that Todd's back from the dead.

TODD. I wasn't dead.

D.N.B. Everyone grab a glass.

> *(**JACK** takes the bottle he's been saving and looks around the room, then at **ALLISON**. This is not the way he imagined this going down. And his audience is not exactly primed for his speech, now, but he nevertheless continues as best he can*

– and if anything, the speech has now taken on an unexpected significance.)

JACK. *(Holding up his "special bottle.")* This bottle. I've been saving this bottle. I tasted this, I don't know, five years ago? It was a little pricey for the restaurant I was working at the time, the owner didn't think he'd be able to shift it at the price point… but I bought this one bottle.

(He holds it up proudly and then sets it down on the table amid several other bottles of wine.)

I had to hide the receipt from Allison. I didn't want her knowing I'd spent our *car payment* on a bottle of wine…she hates extravagance. And obviously she hates birthdays. But I tasted this…and I'm not trying to be corny…but I tasted this and it reminded me of you. *(He smiles at* ALLISON.*)* It is complex, I mean, it's *really* complex… but there's a challenge there, right?

…You don't know exactly what it is you're experiencing… but you want to keep at it. It is full bodied – okay, yeah maybe this is a little corny – but there is an unexpected sweetness that only comes out if you stick with it until the very end. The finish. I need a wine key.

(But TODD *takes over for him, grabbing the bottle.)*

TODD. You talk, I'll open.

*(*TODD *has to look around for the wine key, but when he locates it and picks up the bottle to open it…he has picked up the wrong bottle.* TODD *has inadvertently picked up* DAVID NATHAN BRIGHT*'s gift bottle.)*

JACK. – Easy drinking, goes with anything you're putting on…and there is a memorable *something* that stays with you long after you've tasted even the smallest drop. Okay, that was very corny.

*(*ALLISON, *without warning, has started tearing up. She looks over at* TODD, *smiling through her tears.)*

TODD. *(Trying to pop the cork.)* Oop, she's a stubborn one

JACK. So if you'll get your glasses at the ready…
I will propose this toast to this wonderful woman who –
ALLISON. Todd!

> (**ALLISON** *shrieks.* **TODD** *mistakenly pops the cork on the $6,000 bottle of wine.*)

JACK. – What –??
ALLISON. – Not that –!!
FREYA. – That's –
TODD. – What, what I do –?
ALLISON. The wine David brought.
D.N.B. That's okay.
ALLISON. No. It's not, it's –
FREYA. *(Triumphantly.)* Six thousand dollars a bottle!

TODD.	JACK.
(Wants to say 'Fuck!!', but only air seeps out.) …!	WHAT??

> (**FREYA** *is laughing now like a lunatic, her arms stretched into the air.* **ALLISON** *grabs the opened bottle of wine from* **TODD** *and holds it high above her head like the Holy Grail.*)

JACK. *(To* **TODD***.)* Get her out of here.
TODD. Hey, hey…!

> (**TODD** *helps* **FREYA** *toward the door to escort her out of the room for the bathroom. But she tries to pull away with one final word for* **DAVID NATHAN BRIGHT***.*)

FREYA. Who are you? What do you want?? WHAT DO YOU WANT??
D.N.B. Nothing.
FREYA. That's totally *fucked* up! That's totally *beyond* all comprehension. I'll figure it out. I don't know what it is, I don't know what you're up to pal, but I'm gonna sleuth it out.

> (**TODD** *is insistent now, pulling – or rather,
> dragging – her offstage.*)

TODD. Freya!

> (*She concedes and exits with* **TODD**, *their voices
> trailing off.*)

TODD. You been at that guy all night!

FREYA. Why is he so nice??

> (*A moment, as* **DAVID NATHAN BRIGHT** *looks at*
> **ALLISON**, *then* **JACK**.)

D.N.B. It's fine. Just decant it. We can drink it later. With
Pauline.
I'd like to taste Jack's wine.
That's what I'd like to do.
Wine is about emotion.
And your tasting notes were *remarkable*. Please.
I would be honored to taste your wine.

> (*He holds out his glass.*)

> (**JACK** *stands there for a moment, trying to make
> sense of what has just happened.*)

JACK. Ruined.

ALLISON. Jack?

JACK. Everything's ruined… I wanted to make this moment
special, I really did, in spite of your *admonitions*… I love
you, Allison, I really love you…but Freya's right…this
thing you have – this aversion to birthdays – it's…*selfish.*

ALLISON. Honey, please –

JACK. No, shut up! You're selfish, and it's ruined.

> (*He levels her with his look.* **DAVID NATHAN**
> **BRIGHT** *looks away.* **TODD** *has returned to the
> stage and caught the tone.*)

I don't know how it could get any worse.

> (**JACK***'s phone rings on the table.* **TODD** *answers.*)

TODD. (*Small-as-a-mouse.*) Hello?

Not a good time.

Okay. Hold on.

JACK. Take a message.

TODD. I think you want to take this.

JACK. *Take* a message!

> (**TODD** *holds the phone out to* **ALLISON**, *who takes it.*)

ALLISON. Hi, Jack's indisposed at present. Can I –? Uh-huh.

> (**ALLISON** *listens.*)
>
> (*Five seconds.*)
>
> (**JACK** *knows exactly who's calling and what they're calling about.*)
>
> (**ALLISON** *hangs up.*)

JACK. Let me guess.

ALLISON. We'll talk about it later.

JACK. Did he say why?

Did he give any reason whatsoever?

Did he at least sound…

> (**JACK** *crosses and takes a dish from the table and hurls it against the back wall. He circles the table and throws another of his dishes at the wall with a horrible crash! He pulls the tablecloth off the table and onto the floor. By the time he's finished, the upstage wall of the apartment is bespattered, rather artfully, in haute cuisine.* **ALLISON** *just stands there, a hand covering her mouth in disbelief.* **JACK** *goes to the kitchen.* **ALLISON** *hurriedly follows him out.*)
>
> (**TODD** *stares at the wall of destroyed food, then turns to* **DAVID NATHAN BRIGHT**. *They look at one another awkwardly.* **TODD***'s cell phone chirps one more time.*)

TODD. I just remembered whose umbrella that is. There's

a woman, this older woman. Comes into the dealership couple times a week now for a year. We've been told, we've been warned. She never buys. Just wants to be driven around in one of the cars. She lost her husband a year ago. She's lonely. I don't mind. It gets me out of the showroom for an hour. I drive her around. Like a chauffeur. You know, it's actually quite relaxing… being a chauffeur. I should have thought about that. Driving cars instead of selling them.

I gave her my number. She texts me quite a lot now and we go have a coffee, or, lunch – sometimes we walk around museums. We went to an art museum the other day. I've never really spent time looking at art. It's really interesting…isn't it?

Anyway that's the reason I got fired. But I can't tell Freya that, I can't tell her the truth, she'd think I'd lost my fucking mind. She couldn't possibly conceive I'd sacrifice my livelihood to help out a little old lady.

> (*He looks at* **DAVID NATHAN BRIGHT**.)

I don't know why I told you that.

Anyway. (*Soberly.*) Sorry I puked on you.

> (*The doorbell rings.* **TODD** *looks off.*)

> (**JACK** *and* **ALLISON** *return to the stage.*)

D.N.B. (*To* **TODD**.) I'll get it, we're not staying.

> (**DAVID NATHAN BRIGHT** *reaches into his inside pocket and takes out a checkbook. He takes out a pen. He writes out a check and tears it out of the book.*)

JACK. What are you doing?

D.N.B. It's not a gift.

It's an investment.

> (**JACK** *looks at the check. He looks at* **ALLISON**, *then back at* **DAVID NATHAN BRIGHT**.)

> (*The doorbell rings again.*)

> (**TODD** *heads off to answer the door.*)

D.N.B. *(Cont.)* And, listen: I have this book.
  Cien Sonetos de Amor.
  A first edition.
  I'll have it sent round.
  Neruda's love sonnets.
  It's the perfect gift for both of you.

> *(***DAVID NATHAN BRIGHT*** starts to leave, but* ***JACK****'s face changes. He tears across the room and hits* ***DAVID NATHAN BRIGHT*** *viciously across the face.* ***DAVID NATHAN BRIGHT*** *staggers backward.* ***TODD*** *returns and intervenes.)*

> *(***ALLISON*** screams like a banshee! Her scream has been so shrill, so surprising, that the three men have stopped fighting. She has grabbed* ***DAVID NATHAN BRIGHT****'s gift bottle.)*

> *(***ALLISON*** brandishes the bottle in the air. Then proceeds to guzzle the contents like a mad woman, spilling as much wine down her chin and clothes as she consumes. The three men watch her, frozen in astonishment. And now* ***FREYA*** *has returned to the stage to witness the insanity. As the lights suddenly crossfade into the final scene.)*

Scene Eight

*(The next morning. **DAVID NATHAN BRIGHT**'s apartment – tasteful, extremely minimal. Where the wall of wrecked food once stood in the last scene, a large painting now dominates this final one: Nicolas Poussin's* L'Eté. *It is early morning, and the room is beginning to fill with a golden light. **ALLISON** is asleep on an antique chaise, a blanket thrown over her. **DAVID NATHAN BRIGHT** enters, already dressed for the day. His shirt is crisply pressed, but still untucked. His hand and wrist are wrapped in an Ace bandage, and he has a Band-Aid above his right eye, a cut on his lip. He stands for a moment, watching **ALLISON** sleep, as he sips his morning coffee. **ALLISON** stirs.)*

ALLISON. *(Disoriented.)* Hi.

D.N.B. You fell asleep.

ALLISON. How did that happen?

D.N.B. I imagine because you lay down and closed your eyes.

ALLISON. What happened to you?

> *(He's not sure he wants to tell, but she beats him to the punch.)*

Oh god. I thought I dreamt that.

D.N.B. It's just a sprain.

He tore up the check.

He tried to make me eat it, as I recall.

Although, I don't think it was the money.

It was Neruda.

ALLISON. Can you help me retrace my steps?

D.N.B. You were quite *animated* when you arrived, and more than a little –

ALLISON. Drunk? Was I drunk?

D.N.B. Let's just say, you entered like Eleonora Duse, stood in my doorway, hurling a string of unusually imaginative expletives at me, and proceeded to guzzle the dregs of the bottle of wine I gave you.

ALLISON. Oh god!

D.N.B. – Dribbling most of it down your chin – which I consider the gravest of your sins.

>*(He smiles.)*

ALLISON. Okay, I thought that was part of the dream as well, but that actually happened, did it?

D.N.B. *(Nods.)* You polished off Jack's bottle too. It was horrifying. And adorable. In a horrifying kind of way.
What did you think?
Of the wine, by the way?

ALLISON. I honestly can't remember.

>**(DAVID NATHAN BRIGHT** *laughs generously.)*

D.N.B. I'll bring round another bottle.

ALLISON. I don't deserve it.

D.N.B. You know what's worse than watching someone waste a bottle of really fantastic wine by dousing themselves in it? Drinking it alone.

ALLISON. I found your little card, with your address. I thought, right, I'm going over there, without entirely knowing what I was going to do when I arrived. How did I arrive?
How did I even get into the building?

D.N.B. I considered asking the doorman to rough you up and toss you back onto the street. But Lionel's a bit of a softy.

ALLISON. *(Vaguely.)* I do remember Lionel. I think I remember Lionel. Friendly eyes? Built like a Sherman tank?

D.N.B. That's Lionel.

ALLISON. What happened last night?

D.N.B. Not much. You sort of...

ALLISON. Blacked out?

D.N.B. It was a bit more dignified than that. You were

talking, and then you just *stopped*, slumped over on the chaise here, and that was that. I threw a blanket over you and went to bed. When I came out this morning it looked like you hadn't moved a muscle all night.

> (**ALLISON** *rises and drifts about the room, the blanket still wrapped about her.*)

What was the other part? Of what you thought was a dream?

ALLISON. Oh – that I went to an ATM and took out $80 in cash so I could throw it at you to finally pay you back for lunch.

> (**DAVID NATHAN BRIGHT** *takes $80 in cash out of his pocket and hands it to her.*)

> (**ALLISON** *sighs, ashamedly, and takes back the money.*)

I'm horrible – I will never drink again – I'm leaving.

> (*She begins to stand, but finds herself unsteady on her feet.*)

Okay, maybe a few minutes longer.

> (*She takes in the place for the first time.*)

God, it's beautiful here. All that light.

D.N.B. Isn't it?

ALLISON. You don't have much. I pictured more.

D.N.B. I don't need more.

Can I get you anything?

I'm having coffee.

ALLISON. Please.

And some Tylenol?

> (*He exits, and she takes in the entire room, the painting.*)

(*Calling offstage.*) Are you all alone here?

D.N.B. (*Offstage.*) In the sense no one lives with me, yes. In the sense you're here with me now, no.

> *(He returns to the stage and hands her a coffee, the Tylenol.)*

D.N.B. *(Cont.)* But I'm assuming it wasn't a metaphysical question.

ALLISON. *(Re: the painting.)* Is that –?…what I think it is?

D.N.B. If you think it's a painting, then yes.

ALLISON. Yes, but…*that* painting.

D.N.B. You recognize it.

ALLISON. It's – it's been a very long time.

D.N.B. Poussin.

There's a series.

This one is *L'Eté*.

ALLISON. Summer.

> *(He nods. **ALLISON** moves a little closer, blowing on her hot coffee.)*

D.N.B. She's come to ask him for something.

He holds out his hand, and offers his help.

ALLISON. Ruth. It's Ruth, isn't it? And Boaz.

D.N.B. She knows her artwork *and* her Bible.

ALLISON. "Why have I found such favor in your eyes that you notice me."

D.N.B. It's about redemption.

ALLISON. For her?

D.N.B. And for him.

> *(She turns to him. A moment.)*

Do you want to know a secret?

ALLISON. *(Lets out a sigh.)* You're going to share a secret? David, I know nothing about you. You're the most mysterious person I've ever met. Despite the interrogation everyone put you through last night – you're *now* suddenly going to offer up a secret without any prodding?

D.N.B. Oh all right, then, I'll just read the paper.

> *(He starts out, jokingly.)*

ALLISON. No. No, yes, please. Please, I want to know a secret.

>   *(He looks at her and smiles, then looks at the Poussin.)*

D.N.B. It's a knock-off.

ALLISON. Shut up. This is a fake?

D.N.B. The ones you passed in the entryway are the real McCoy, but this…*fake.* The owner wanted to have the original, but, you know…

ALLISON. Too expensive?

D.N.B. No. They wouldn't let her.

ALLISON. What?

D.N.B. *Have* it –

ALLISON. – Who wouldn't?

D.N.B. The *Louvre.*

They're a bit snobby that way.

So instead of, you know, nicking it from the museum and bringing Interpol down on her…she, uh…she had this one commissioned.

>   *(**ALLISON** moves closer to inspect the painting.)*

He was just a kid

The painter. At the time.

Twenty-two, but showed promise, and was encouraged.

Two days before he started work on it, he sustained a fracture to his right hand. She thought: it's going to be weeks before he can start painting again, *if* he can start. So she asked him, she said, How did it happen? He said, Oh, you know, I just had to slam it a couple times in the car door.

ALLISON. He'd done it to himself.

>   *(He nods.)*

D.N.B. Poussin. He experienced tremors. Of the hand. Toward the end of his life. It took him an extraordinary amount of time to complete this work, and would have likely been very painful.

The painter…well, he was a just foolish kid, wasn't he? He wanted it to be authentic.

ALLISON. It's breathtaking.

D.N.B. Unfortunately…

> *(And here he draws in a half-breath.)*

…my wife didn't live long enough to appreciate the product of his dedication.

> *(There is a moment of silence, here, the two of them just looking at the painting quietly, side-by-side. Then* **DAVID NATHAN BRIGHT** *takes out another check from his pocket and holds it out to her.)*

Here is another check.

Which I will expect you to cash.

And in return, Allison, listen to me…*look* at me…in return I want absolutely nothing.

ALLISON. I can't –

D.N.B. Jack needs it.

He deserves it. He has talent. All he needs is a fair break. Don't take it for yourself. Do it for him.

> *(He places the check on the pillow upon which she slept.)*

Do you need anything else?

What I meant was: why did you come?

ALLISON. I don't know why.

D.N.B. I think you do.

You came to tell me something. Didn't you?

ALLISON. No.

D.N.B. Then why come?

ALLISON. I came here –

D.N.B. Yes.

ALLISON. I came here to tell you –

D.N.B. Yes, what?

ALLISON. Whatever it is you want from me, name it – there is nothing that I will not give you, at this point, in order to repay my debt. In order –

D.N.B. Your debt?

ALLISON. – in order to release myself.

D.N.B. Nothing?

ALLISON. Nothing at all. What do you want?

Please.

Tell me.

What do you want from me? Because, because –

D.N.B. I think it's you. I think it's you who wants something desperately from me. Or, perhaps, we both want the same thing.

ALLISON. Look – if you're just going to be cryptic…

(**ALLISON** *sets down her cup and starts for the door, but his voice stops her dead in her tracks.*)

D.N.B. There are people who give expecting something in return. They extort loyalty, obeisance, they want the receiver genuflecting in perpetuity. That's not a gift, it's…enslavement.

Generosity is giving away so much of yourself that you eventually…disappear. You ask me what I want: that's all I want. To disappear.

(**ALLISON** *is absolutely frozen now, unable to leave, terrified of staying.*)

Release yourself from what?

(*Brief pause.*)

You're a twin. Allison.

Isn't that what you told me? In the park?

You have a twin brother.

So your birthday, is *his* birthday.

(*She has to inhale here, but is unable to get a full breath.*)

Release yourself from what?

(**ALLISON** *has finished her coffee long ago, but now she tightly grips her cup and looks into it expecting, hoping, to find some answer to what she needs to say next.*)

ALLISON. My brother…he, you know the stereotype of twins, so close, so connected. That was never us. We waged a vicious war from the time we were young. It devastated our mother.

(**DAVID NATHAN BRIGHT** *is just quietly listening. She knows she must either go on, or she must leave immediately, and he's offering nothing in the way of an inducement in either direction.*)

We had very different values, radically different, but more than that…apart from everything else, he was cruel. Unforgivably cruel, to me, to everyone, and he lived…a sinful life.

When we were kids, nine, maybe ten, he gave me this little paperweight, cobalt blue. I treasured it. It turned out he'd stolen it – a friend of my mother – he'd taken it from her bedroom and gave it to me for my birthday. My mother made me return it to the woman, who naturally assumed I was the one who'd stolen it. I didn't have the heart to tell her it was my brother. She regarded me with such disdain that I felt myself like the thief. And after a time, I started to believe it.

For years, I swallowed the guilt for all my brother's transgressions. I hated him so much, but I ate his sins… in exchange for getting him out of my life.

(*The sunlight is lengthening across the floor now.*)

He was in Malaysia when he got sick. Who knows why? We hadn't spoken in years, so I learned all this *after* the fact, *after* it was too late to…

He called.

But I didn't answer.

For months he called.

Again and again.

So I changed my number.

And then: my mother called.

My brother died…alone…in agony…on our birthday… in a hospital in Penang. *(Beat.)* He was calling for something only I could give: bone marrow. *(Beat.)* But I never bothered to pick up the phone.

> *(She looks at him now, desperate for a response, imploring:)*

Aren't you going to say something? It would make things easier, this isn't easy, this is hard, really fucking hard. So if you have anything to offer in the way of help, this would be the time.

> *(But **DAVID NATHAN BRIGHT** still says nothing. What he does do: he slowly extends his open hand to her, an offering. **ALLISON**, hesitant at first, cautiously makes her way toward him. And here, she involuntarily kneels before him.)*

A week after his death I received a package in the mail. It was the paperweight. I have no idea when or how or even if he'd stolen it back again from that neighbor, but it was yet again in my possession. The un-generous gift. This horrible little token of his – my selfishness. And a note: "Happy birthday."

> *(The sunlight has finally reached the place where she has knelt.)*

I went into the street and gave the paperweight to the first person I saw.

> *(**DAVID NATHAN BRIGHT** sits looking at her in silence. **ALLISON** kisses **DAVID NATHAN BRIGHT**'s hand.)*

ALLISON. Thank you.

D.N.B. It's nothing.

> *(They turn to the painting, as the light from the windows strikes the Poussin, illuminating the central figures that are the subject of the*

composition. Five seconds. **DAVID NATHAN BRIGHT** *stands. He disappears.* **ALLISON** *is alone, she stands. She turns toward us. She sees the check. She looks out at the audience. Five seconds. Blackout.)*